ONE HOT SUMMER

DEBBIE IOANNA

Print ISBN: 978-1-917214-20-9

PROLOGUE

Zante
10 Years Earlier...

I pulled Sarah's groping hands out of my bikini top.

"Will you stop? Everyone will think we're lesbians! Which I wouldn't mind, except we're not!" The resort was quite busy at that moment, with the arrival of other fellow university students ready to kick off their summer break.

"That's not a bad thing! We've just finished our final year, we need to let our hair down." She finally took her seat beside me.

"Hair down, yes." I put myself back in place. "Boobs out, no."

Sarah ignored me as she observed our mainly male audience who weren't exactly being subtle. "Look at them all. Soak it all up while you can." She whipped her hair behind her shoulders and leaned back in her chair, using her suitcase as a footrest to show off her freshly waxed legs. "Anyway, I'm just trying to give you a little more cleavage. Pull them up yourself. You've got great boobs. Show 'em off."

"I don't see why we had to put our bikinis on, we haven't even been given our room key yet." I was feeling very self-conscious sitting in such a public place in a bikini top. Sarah had let me keep my shorts on, for now. It wouldn't be long until she was insisting my legs were out in the sun too, although surely that would be a danger to planes flying over, in the same way you shouldn't shine lasers into the sky. My legs hadn't seen daylight in quite some time.

We had been waiting for our holiday rep since arriving, but he was being held hostage by an angry older couple at the hotel entrance, so had told us all to wait in the outdoor dining area. Sarah relaxed in her chair, whereas I was using my bag to hide my belly. This was not a flattering position. I would have preferred to be laid flat out on a sun lounger, rather than beached on a plastic dining chair, which was making me sweat already. Every time I leaned forward, I could feel my skin peeling itself away from the plastic.

"Fancy a dip in the pool? We can really drive them wild."

"No, I don't!"

"Come on, Jenny, you promised you'd loosen up on this trip. Live a little. We're twenty-one! Uni is done, this is the start of our last summer of freedom. Start to relax."

"I will, I will, just not yet. I want to unpack and figure out where I'm sleeping tonight. Get my bearings. Once I've done that, I'll feel better."

"It'll be fine, we're up there somewhere." She pointed to the rooms looking over us. "Just relax."

The basic, rectangular pool took centre stage, surrounded by sun loungers and small tables. I could see a bar on one side, and a restaurant on the other. I counted four floors of apartments in between, all with towels flung carelessly over the balconies.

Some stripey, spotty or sporting various Premier League football team logos. The whole place was enclosed by a ten-foot-high white concrete wall, which made me feel very secure. I'd never been on holiday without my parents before. I could always rely on Dad to have his watchful eye on me, but he can't do that all the way from Halifax. *We* were the grown-ups on this trip, responsible for our own safety and well-being.

"Hiya, guys!" Our very animated Scouser rep finally appeared, with his clipboard in his right hand, and his left hand floating in the air as though he was holding onto an invisible cigarette. "Right, so sorry about the delay, oof, it's warm today, innit? Well, everyone, I'm Gareth, but please call me Gaz." There were about twenty of us who had all disembarked off the rickety coach to stay at Arizona Apartments. Not one person looked over the age of twenty-one. "Okay, I see you ladies couldn't wait to get started on the tan." He winked at us. "So, we're just about ready now. If you make your way to reception, we can get started."

"Finally." I was getting hungry. It was nearly five o'clock back home and we had not eaten since our pre-flight Burger King this morning. I had no idea what the local time was, but I definitely needed a sandwich or something.

Sarah stood. "I say we grab our keys, dump our bags in the room, and come straight back down. Get some pool action before the sun disappears."

"Well..."

"I know you want to unpack, but we can do that later. It looks like the bar serves light snacks and brings them to you while you're sunbathing. We can have a light bite now and eat properly later."

"I guess we could." Looking over to the bar, I could see bags of Lay's crisps in all flavours in a basket.

"Yes, we can. You look so good in that bikini."

"I don't feel it." I blushed, holding my arms across my stomach, feeling far too exposed. "I'm just not used to this."

"I know, but I promise, you look fab. How do I look?"

"Absolutely stunning." She *always* looked good. Even when our alarms woke us up at three o'clock this morning, her face had looked like it always did. Unlike my own face, which was marked by my fingers as I'd fallen asleep leaning on my hand.

"Aww, thanks babes." She bounced forward, kissing me on the cheek. "Come on, let's get in the queue for our room keys."

As soon as we had our keys, we were up to the second floor, looking for our room. Sarah found it in no time. I didn't even get a foot in the door before she pulled my suitcase from me and shoved it inside, quickly locking the door again.

"Can't we look around?"

"Yes, later. Come on, let's get back down to the pool! I spotted some free sun loungers. I wonder if those guys are still there."

They were. There were four guys all sitting together. Two of them were being straddled by two girls in string bikinis, leaving very little to the imagination. This left two singletons who were very interested in us as we approached. In between swigging their beers and puffing on cigarettes, they kept looking our way.

A waiter appeared with a tray of various colourful drinks as we arranged our sun loungers so we could be comfortable.

"Would you like a complimentary cocktail, ladies?" he asked. Sarah picked up two, which resembled piña coladas, and handed one to me.

"Thank you," I said to the waiter, as he went on his way to

offer the rest of the drinks to the other new arrivals who'd had the same idea as us.

"So, we need a plan of action." Sarah sipped on her cocktail and turned to face me. "Eugh, there's barely any alcohol in that. Anyway, plan of action. We're only here for a week, so we need to make the most of it."

"I'm sure the rep could give us some idea of day trips. I read there are some good old town markets nearby and there might be a zoo. We could–"

"No, not day trips, you spoon. I'm talking about fun. We just worked our arses off for our exams, and we're about to enter the exciting world of adulthood. This is our last chance to go wild!"

Sarah slurped on her cocktail, finishing it in seconds.

"Well, that was gross, I'm going to get us some real drinks. Be right back and then we can plan."

She grabbed her bag and ran across to the bar. She leaned across the counter to get the waiter's attention and was served in no time. I looked around while I waited. The sun was still hot, but getting low in the sky, so I had to shield my eyes with my hands, hoping that my sunglasses were in my suitcase and not in the kitchen drawer at my mother's house.

"I knew you'd forget something," I could hear her saying.

I looked across at the group of guys. One of them looked at me at the same time. My eyes quickly darted away. *Why am I so shy?* I looked back and he was still looking at me. He smiled and then lifted his hand to give me a small wave. I smiled back. He was quite good-looking. Very tanned too, so he must have been here a while already.

"Finally, here. Drink this."

Sarah handed me a small tumbler, which had the look of cola, but with one sip I could tell it was almost pure vodka.

"Yep," she laughed at my sour expression, "no water in *this*. Drink up!"

It didn't take long for the watered-down cocktail and almost pure vodka to start to settle in my empty stomach. I could hear club music playing in the distance, and suddenly felt the urge to dance.

"We need to find some kind of club or something."

"Yes! That's the spirit." She held out her glass and loudly called out, "Girls on tour!"

"Woo, girls on tour!"

"Girls on tour!" we said again in unison.

We clinked glasses and giggled as the two single guys held up their drinks to us and cheered. It was true – we had worked bloody hard over the last few months. I'd barely seen Sarah, even though we had been living together in our own very tiny student flat. She might have been my crazy best friend, but once she got her study head on, she was unapproachable. That's if you could find her. However, once the pressure was off, she more than made up for it, and we always had the most memorable times.

As the sun went down and the dark fell, the lights around the pool came on and guided us back to the stairs, helping us to avoid falling into the water. Balance was becoming an issue after Sarah had insisted on a few more vodkas.

"Come on," Sarah slurred. "We can have a quick shower, freshen up and then try the restaurant. Have some food, refuel, then head out. What do you think?"

"Sounds like a plan. I am starving." I gripped the banister with both hands as I had almost tripped on the second step. "I thought they were supposed to water down the drinks here. That vodka was actual, pure vodka."

"Mine too, we've barely eaten though. We should've

grabbed some crisps. A splash of cold water and we'll be... Oh, hello."

I looked up to see the two singletons alongside us on the stairs.

"Hello." His accent was instantly recognisable. "Where are you girls from?"

"Yorkshire," I said, trying to focus my eyes on the swaying Essex boy. Although I was finding it difficult to focus properly, I could just make out his green eyes.

"Oh, I love Yorkshire." He smiled.

"Is that right?" I laughed. "And if we were from Newcastle, I bet you'd love that too."

"Absolutely."

"Ignore my friend," Sarah said. "She's not into cheesy chat-up lines."

"Oh yeah? How about you?" asked Essex number two.

"You can try me." She twirled her hair between her fingers, looking up at him.

"Well, how about this." He put his hands on his hips, accepting the challenge. "Your blonde hair is beautiful, is it natural–"

"No," she said quickly before he could finish his line. "It's supernatural. Don't upset me or it might curse you."

"Ha!" Both Essex boys laughed. "I'm Jamie," said Sarah's daring love interest. "This is my pal, Joe. Aren't you girls sticking around for the party?"

"What party?" Sarah asked.

"The hotel is throwing a big bash tonight, big pool party. It's gonna be mint. Kicks off in a few minutes. Are you coming back down?"

"We might be, we could be convinced." Sarah winked at me.

"We'll see you back down there then, I hope."

I blushed as Joe gave me one last smile before heading back down to their spot by the pool.

"Oh my God, Sarah!" I said when they were out of earshot. "They want us to join them. What are we wearing tonight? Will you do my make-up? Are we going to the party?"

"Of course we're going," she hooked her arm around mine, "but we don't need to get changed. It's a pool party, we're fine as we are. Come on."

A few hours later, we were still sitting by the pool with our Essex boys, and things were progressing very quickly. Cocktail after cocktail was being consumed, and the more I drank, the more X-rated the situation was becoming. This was very out of character for me, but there was something about the beautiful setting, being with my best friend, a few drinks and the fact that the stress of university life and dissertations were over that made me want to have fun. The boys had told us they were leaving tomorrow, which spurred us on to make the night even more exciting.

"Why don't we move the party upstairs?" I heard Jamie suggest to Sarah.

"I suppose we could," Sarah teased. "To your room?"

"We can't, it's shared with the others, and I suspect it might get... overcrowded. They've been a nightmare all week. How about yours?"

"We could do. Hey, Jenny?"

"Yeah?"

"We're going up, private party. You guys coming?"

I looked at Joe. We had been talking for quite some time, and I really liked him. He had just finished university too and was having one final holiday with his friends before venturing to

Australia for a year of travelling on his own. I had never had a one-night stand, ever, but he was too good to let go. Essex was a million miles away, so it was not like I could just hop on the bus to visit him in the future. It was now or never.

"How about it?" I asked, fearful he would turn me down, even now.

"Yes, if you're sure. What's your place like? Do you two have separate rooms?"

"Well, I don't know, to be honest. I was too eager to get back down to this party. I remember seeing a bed, but have no idea if there was another bed through another door, or if there even was another door for that matter. I think it's only one bedroom, but there's a balcony we can chill on, although I'm not sure if there's any furniture." It was still warm outside, so no reason we couldn't sit out.

"Well, we can find out?" Joe reached for my hand and pulled me up so we could follow Sarah and Jamie up to our room. I was glad Joe had hold of me. My lack of food almost resulted in a midnight dip in the pool.

"Here we are!" Sarah opened the door to our room and I could finally have a proper look around... although there wasn't much to look at.

"Sarah, didn't you request separate beds?" It looked as though we were about to get very close for the next seven nights, although I wasn't particularly keen on a foursome tonight. I peeked my head in the door to my right, finding a shower room with a sink and toilet. Not even a bath to chill out in. There were no other rooms, this was it. A queen-sized bed and a small two-seater sofa.

Joe walked around the bed and opened up the balcony doors.

"Your balcony isn't a bad size, it's almost bigger than the actual room. We could pull the couch out here."

I joined him by the double doors. I didn't want to upset the managers by dragging furniture outside. One glance behind me at Sarah and Jamie smooching on the bed quickly changed my mind though. Joe and I managed to pull the couch out, and closed the door behind us, leaving Sarah and Jamie to it.

"We'll leave them alone for a while I think." Joe seemed embarrassed by his friend, or perhaps gutted that he didn't get to the bed first. "So, you've got a *very* nice view."

I laughed as I looked out into the darkness. I could hear waves crashing into an invisible beach, but had no idea where it was, or what our room was looking onto. I guessed nothing as there were no lights to be seen anywhere, besides the one shining down on us. It was a very private balcony.

"Shall we..." I hesitated. "Do you want to sit down?"

"It'd be rude not to, seeing as though I made you drag it out here with me." He laughed as we sat down together. I suddenly had butterflies in my very empty tummy. I felt like a fifteen-year-old girl about to kiss her first boy. Sarah had said I was shy with guys, and I guess I was, but only with guys that I liked.

"So, you said you were leaving tomorrow. What time do you need to go?" I was struggling to find something interesting to talk about. The more he looked into my eyes, the more I panicked. *Has my make-up smudged? Do I look fat?*

"Early," he said, looking down at my lips, getting closer to my face.

"So, you'll be needing an early night... right?"

"Yeah, I probably should..."

As soon as his lips met mine, there was no stopping us. Clothes, the small amount we had on, were pulled off. Things moved very fast. Luckily, that tiny amount of soberness still inside me made sure he had a condom, which he pulled out of his pocket and put on whilst I glanced out into the darkness on the other side of the railings.

This was it. My first one-night stand. Popping my Zante cherry.

We found ourselves competing with the noises coming from inside, not caring that there were rooms on either side of us, or lights shining down on us. After all, this was a very private balcony. After a few surprisingly satisfying minutes, we fell asleep together, still interlocked and naked.

~

Tap, tap.

Jamie's knocking on the glass door woke us up. Sober, and cold, I used Joe's shirt to cover myself up. The sky was orange as the sun was coming up across the way, and shining directly onto us, but I couldn't focus on anything. The sudden light was hurting my sensitive eyes. A holiday hangover was not intended so soon.

"Mate, we should go. Coach'll be here soon." Jamie slid the door open. He stretched as he yawned. "Got to go grab our bags."

"Comin' mate." Joe rubbed his eyes and quickly put his pants on. I stepped inside, picking up a neatly rolled towel, which had fallen to the floor, and wrapped it around me, handing Joe his shirt back. "Thanks. So, do you want to swap numbers or something?"

It might have been nice, but given the distance and his upcoming venture to the other side of the world, I felt there was probably no point.

"No, don't worry about that. I hope you have a great time in Australia."

"It was nice meeting you," he said, blushing as he smiled at me. "Make sure you enjoy the rest of your holiday, Yorkshire girl."

I allowed him to kiss me, but the confidence I'd had the previous night was long gone and I didn't want to look at him. I just wanted to climb into bed. Once the balcony and room doors were closed, and both guys had left, I climbed in and joined Sarah in a long, dehydrated, hung-over sleep.

Bang, bang.

Either my head was about to implode, or someone was at the door. I hoped it was the latter, although it felt like the former.

"Jenny…" Sarah's weak voice called out. "Jenny, the door."

"I know." I could barely lift my head off the pillow.

Bang, Bang.

"Hang on," she called to the impatient visitors whilst struggling to sit up. "Goddam cleaners."

"Not today!" I shouted at the door.

"Can you let me in, girls?" Gaz's unmistakable voice called through the door. "We need to talk."

"What does he want?" I asked.

"Hopefully telling us we were given the wrong room and that we're being relocated." She flung back the bedsheet and threw on her kaftan. "I'm coming," she called.

I readjusted my towel to make sure I was covered when Gaz walked in, accompanied by a man in a suit, making me quickly jump out of the bed.

"What's going on?" Sarah asked.

"This is Mr Martinez, the hotel manager. It seems, ah, there was a complaint made to the hotel this morning." Although Gaz used a serious tone when speaking to us, there was something about his lips that suggested he wanted to laugh. "Was someone out on the balcony last night?"

I could feel my face burning up, as Gaz followed the manager across the room, heading to the sliding patio doors.

"Oh, right, well…" I looked at Sarah, who was blushing too.

"Well, I have a complaint of my own." Sarah crossed her

arms and looked at the manager. "We have been given the wrong room. I specifically booked a twin room with a separate living area. This is just ridiculous. No wonder one of us was forced to sleep outside."

"Well, from the nature of the complaint, there wasn't much sleeping going on." Gaz's eyes looked at mine and then eyed something on the floor of the balcony. It was the used condom. I wanted to die on the spot. The manager took one look at the condom, nodded at Gaz and then stomped out of the room, slamming the door behind him. "I'm so sorry, girls, but you have to leave."

"What?" we said together.

"Do you see the house opposite yours?" He pointed across. "That *massive* villa right in front of you?"

"Oh, well, yes…" I said, seeing the view clearly for the first time. The villa was barely five metres from our room, and it was huge. Quite hard to miss, actually.

"You put on quite a show last night! And unfortunately for you, that villa is owned by one of the richest families in Europe."

"Really?" Sarah asked, peeking outside. "Who are they?"

"I'm not allowed to tell you, but let's just say they own a very popular football club, and they're staying with their very young children at the moment and have put in a complaint to the resort, making all kinds of threats."

"What? You're pulling my leg. There's no way…"

Gaz pulled out his phone. "My manager's calling, hang on. Hello? Yeah, yeah. I'm with them now, yeah. All right. No, no, no police. No. No! Yeah. Yeah. All right. Yeah. Fab, mate. Sound. That's fab. I'll tell them."

"Police?" I could feel the colour draining from my face. "The police are coming?"

This was it. I was going to be charged with public

indecency. I'd be thrown into a foreign prison. Three years working towards my degree would be in the bin, my future down the drain because of one night letting my hair down.

"No, they've managed to negotiate. It's fine. Well, it *will* be fine once we get you out of here. Pack your things, quickly."

"Wait, is this going to be on the news?" Police or not, if this ended up on the news for all my family to see, I'd be done for. My mother would be shipping me off to a convent.

"Luckily for you, no. It's being dealt with. Come on, get your things, I'll meet you at the bottom of the stairs. There's a taxi here to take you to the airport. My manager has secured you two seats on a flight back to Manchester this morning. He's emailing the tickets over, so I'll go get them printed while you get sorted."

Gaz rushed out of the room, leaving the two of us staring at each other in disbelief.

"Is this real?" I asked. "Is this really happening?"

"I think so. Wow. We know how to party."

I didn't think I'd be planning a return trip to Zante, or anywhere abroad with Sarah, ever again.

Ever.

CHAPTER ONE

PRESENT DAY

My legs straddled Zack's naked body. He was handcuffed to my bed, totally at my mercy. I was in absolute control of this man. My man. He was finally mine. The cuffs dug in to his wrists as he struggled between pain and pleasure.

"Do you want me to stop?" I asked over his cries of passion as I kissed his chest, working my way down his torso. His body was trembling beneath mine as the excitement built.

"No," Zack cried out. "Oh, Jenny, no, keep doing that."

As I finally gave in to his body's demands, I climbed back on top of him and we began to move together, quickly. The headboard banged against the wall, making the bed vibrate beneath us. We both moaned as things began to feel good.

"Jenny..." he called out, loudly.

"Yeah," I said, feeling my orgasm about to rip through me as he said my name. "Oh, yeah."

The room seemed to shake as the bed bounced harder and harder.

"Jenny!" He said it louder, but firmer. Not like someone who was enjoying themselves.

"Yeah?" I asked.

"Jenny!" he shouted, with a more feminine voice...

"Jenny!?" Sarah's voice bellowed at me as I finally opened my eyes. "For God's sake, will you wake up from your bloody sex dreams? The plane has landed."

Flushed, I surveyed my surroundings, aware that everyone around me would have heard my nocturnal rendezvous with my absent boyfriend. Other passengers had begun to crowd the aisles of the narrow plane. The ones who weren't staring at me, giggling at Sarah's wake-up call, were getting their coats and bags from the overhead storage as the stewardesses looked on in frustration. People were always in a rush to grab their things once the plane landed, but I never could understand why. It's not like our luggage is ever waiting for us as soon as we exit. I could guarantee it would be another hour before we would leave the airport.

"How long was I snoozing?" I asked Sarah, rubbing my eyes and hoping I wasn't making too many sexual noises in my sleep.

"I'm not sure. A while. How can you even sleep on a plane? It's so uncomfortable." She rubbed her neck. "And how on earth did you manage to sleep through a plane landing? Couldn't you feel us being thrown about? It was quite rough."

I laughed to myself. "I guess I'm just naturally gifted at being able to sleep anywhere." I stretched out my arms, and my elbows clicked. I didn't want to tell her I was exhausted because Zack and I had been up all the night before having wild sex to prepare for not seeing each other for the next few days. We had not been apart for this long in the nine months we'd been together. "I can't wait to get up and stretch my legs. Three hours is a long time to sit still. I'm bursting for a wee."

"You could have just used the airplane loos, you know. You didn't need to hold it in all this time."

"I don't use airplane loos," I said, thinking back to the first time I had attempted it. We were on our shameful flight home from Zante where the previous night's alcohol intake came back with a vengeance and I was violently vomiting my insides into the plane toilets. Sarah thought I was insane when I told her I was sure I could feel air blowing on my face from the loo itself. I got paranoid I was going to get sucked out. After that, a fear of aeroplane facilities took over and I have never dared to use them again. Long haul flights were out of the question.

"Look, you're thirty-one now. I think it's perfectly acceptable to put irrational fears to one side, and have a bloody wee on a plane."

"And get sucked out through the plumbing when I flush it? No thanks."

"Shut up." I nudged her with my shoulder as she laughed. It was great hearing her laugh. It had been a rough time for her, and this holiday would be the distraction she needed.

We were eventually let off the plane. We followed the crowd through the airport via the hour-long queues at passport control, a quick visit to the toilets, and then finally to find our luggage, which was already spinning on the carousel when we arrived.

"Oh, mine, mine, sorry, excuse me." Sarah politely pushed past an older couple to grab her bag, which was making its way around to the other side, grabbing it just in time. Mine wasn't too far behind.

"Well, that went smoothly," she observed as we wheeled our cases to the exit.

"A sign of good times ahead," I promised as we stepped out into the Italian air. The sun was shining down, and the sky was a clear sea of blue. "I don't think it's too far from here into Rome itself. Do you want to attempt the train or get a taxi?"

"Let's get a taxi," Sarah said. "It'll be easier, and we can figure out the public transport system later."

We made our way over to the first taxi that was waiting in

the rank. I showed the driver the slip of paper with our hotel details on.

"Can you take us there, please?"

"*Prego, prego!*" he said, helping to put our luggage into the boot of the car, and gesturing for us to take our seats.

"What did he call you?" Sarah laughed as we climbed into the back seats together, and it wasn't long until we were on our way.

If it were possible to eat a smell, then I would have been munching on the air. As we drove through the roads of Rome with the windows down, one nostril was overdosing on freshly ground coffee and the other was having a foodgasm from freshly cooked pizza dough. I had officially reached food heaven.

Sarah and I arrived at our hotel after a somewhat terrifying taxi ride from the airport. We should have just taken the train like every other tourist who values their life. I'm surprised the doors didn't fall off their hinges as we hit a cobbled street, and the driver definitely overcharged us.

Despite the cost of the taxi, there were to be no expenses spared on this holiday. Seeing as this June weekend should have been Sarah's wedding to Max The Wanker, we decided to splash out over the next few days so the month of June will never need to be *as* tainted by heartbreaking memories. We had a full plan for this break. Sarah would have a wonderful time, even if it killed me. Judging from previous holiday experiences with Sarah, I'm not exaggerating.

We were staying at a small, family-run hotel at the edge of the centre of Rome. The elderly owner Leonardo was approximately four feet tall, and the cutest little Italian man I had ever met. He had a permanent smile on his olive-skinned face, with a bushy moustache that circled around his mouth. His shiny, bald head reflected the sun, and it did not seem to matter how hot it was, he wore a clean white shirt buttoned to the top, and a silver tie pinned to his shirt. His wife Maria was just as tiny as her husband, but as terrifying as a tiger that hadn't eaten for days. She was like a yappy Yorkshire terrier snapping at your feet. A floral scarf was hiding her hair and she wore a matching apron, making her look like the Italian equivalent of Nora Batty. She handed us biscotti as we arrived, which we felt obliged to eat in front of her, fearing we would be scolded if we refused.

"Mmmm," I said, as I tried to crunch down on the hard biscuit without breaking my teeth, "delicious." I wondered if my travel insurance would cover dental emergencies.

"*Si, delizioso!*" she barked, before muttering something in Italian to her husband and walking heavy-footed through another door. We all jumped as we heard the biscotti tray being banged down on a worktop.

"My wife, ah," Leonardo began. I loved his accent. "She will bring coffee to your room, so you can settle." He smiled, as though he was the most content man on earth.

"Oh, that sounds great," Sarah said, "but we really want to go straight back out to explore."

"Yeah, it's still only early, so we thought we'd go for a wander before dinner."

"Ah, wonder?" He looked confused.

"A wander, you know, like a walk around, to see what is nearby."

"Ah, okay, si, si. Here, your key." He handed us an old, rustic key with a tag showing the number '4', dangling on a very fragile piece of string. "Up a-the stair, left," he gestured, "your room at end of corridor."

"Thank you!" We both smiled, but Leonardo looked worried.

"I ah, I go tell Maria we no need coffee."

He anxiously shuffled down to the door Maria went through, and I suddenly felt very guilty.

"Do you think she'll go mad?" I asked Sarah. "I feel awful."

"If he's made it to a hundred years old and she's not killed him yet then I think he'll be okay. Come on, let's get these bags away so we can go back out into the sun."

Sarah and I grabbed our things and headed up the stairs, following Leonardo's directions. The carpet looked as old as Leonardo and his wife, the walls looked aged and the ceiling paint was peeling off, but somehow it did not matter. It looked chic, as though it was intentionally decorated that way. Unlike the peeling paint and damp stains in my own bathroom back at home that I keep putting off fixing. DIY is not my forte, as Zack is quickly learning.

We unlocked our door and walked into our room, which would be our home for the next few nights. We were not disappointed. The air conditioning in particular was a welcome treat. The floor tiles were a deep orange colour, very Mediterranean. There were two single beds covered in clean white bedding, with mustard-yellow cushions and throws, and the curtains hanging in the windows matched it all nicely. It all looked quite modern, which was a surprise. Even the bible by the side of each bed looked like a new edition.

The tall window turned out to be a glass door leading to a small balcony, just big enough for a small round table and two chairs. It would be a squeeze to get us both out there without fear of being pushed over the railings, but I'm sure we would manage... whilst sober.

In the corner of the room was a two-seater sofa with a black metal coffee table in front of it. On top of the table was a plate with yet more biscotti, and a small laminated note was propped up against an ice bucket, which was chilling a bottle of prosecco.

Sarah picked up the note, and read it out in her best attempt at an Italian accent.

"Welcome dear guests to La Casa di Angelo.

We hope you enjoy your stay with us, and your time in Rome.

Breakfast will be brought to your room at 7.30am, which can be eaten on balcony.

Ask for Leonardo if have any problem.

Grazie."

"Perfecto." Sarah smiled, resuming her normal Yorkshire accent. "Breakfast in bed." She put the note back on the table, opened the door to the balcony, and stepped out.

"I'm just going to use the loo," I lied. "I'll be back in a tick."

I had switched my phone on at the airport, but it had not connected to the local network while we were there. I had promised Sarah a phone-free holiday, but I had to check on both of my boys.

There was a WhatsApp message waiting for me with a photo of my two favourite men. The one that cuddles me at night, keeps me warm and makes me feel needed. And the other, the boyfriend of mine that I just can't get enough of. Okay, yes, he cuddles me at night too, but on the rare nights we are not together, I have Bing to keep me company.

> Hope you've arrived, baby, we miss you already xxxx

In the photo, Zack and Bing were lying on my couch. Bing was asleep on Zack's bare chest. *Oh, what I wouldn't give to be there right now.* I can't believe that I am jealous of my cat. My dream from my aeroplane nap has left me very, very horny. I hope Sarah doesn't catch me dry-humping my pillow in my sleep. I fired off a quick reply.

> We're here! It's so hot!! Gorgeous, though.
> Can't wait for pizza. I'll try not to come back
> the size of a whale: PS. Love you Xxxx

Knock knock.

"Have you fallen asleep in there?" Sarah called from the other side of the door. "Let me in, I need a wee."

I opened the door, and she saw the phone in my hand.

"You don't need to hide your phone, you spoon. You're allowed to communicate with your boyfriend."

She sat on the toilet and I admired the bathroom, running my hand along the bath.

"It's all marble," I observed. "Marble floor, tiles, bath, sink, everything."

"I know, it's gorgeous. Nice and cool in here, too."

It was. The air conditioning seemed to have been working very nicely. I walked out of the bathroom, past the beds and out to the balcony, where the heat hit me. Our room faced another building, so there was not much of a view. It was a very narrow street, so there was no breeze coming in through the door either, making it very humid.

In hot, humid weather, there are two types of girls. There are the girls who can wear their long hair free-flowing and held back out of their eyes with their sunglasses on top of their head. They can also have a full face of make-up, without the risk of a sweaty upper lip and panda eyes from mascara melt. Hot, sunny weather suits them. Sarah falls into this category. And then there are the other girls. The ones whose hair sticks to their sun-creamed shoulders so it needs to be tied back in a boring, unflattering ponytail. They can't wear foundation, as the sweat causes it to streak down their faces. Any attempt at eyeliner, and they look like Uncle Fester from the Addams Family. Their upper lips sweat profusely, and they can't walk around in skirts because their legs chafe. Unfortunately for me, I fall into this category of women. I was made for cold winters, snuggled in fluffy blankets and slipper socks.

"That's better." Sarah squeezed next to me on the balcony. "Where shall we go first? Shall we just go for a walk and then find somewhere to eat? I know you're dying for an authentic pizza cooked by actual Italians, and not from the frozen food section at Tesco."

"I'm in Italy, this is my dream come true!" I said, fanning myself with a tissue I found in my pocket. "Pizza is top of my list of things to do. Sightseeing comes later. Pizza over Pisa."

"Okay, let's freshen up and head out before Maria brings us more biscotti."

Back inside, I dug my little bag out of my suitcase and transferred over some necessities for walking around in a hot, foreign country. My little handheld fan would be coming everywhere with me, I do love a fan. I made sure to have a few euros too, just in case some places didn't accept card payment. You never know. Once we were ready, we headed out of the room and downstairs. There was a lot of banging and raised voices in the background. We could make out Maria shouting. Poor Leonardo. Perhaps I could sneak him into my suitcase to bring home with me.

We stepped out of the door, through what felt like a heat curtain, and out onto the cobbled street. Maria's rage could no longer be heard.

"So," Sarah said. "Where shall we go first?"

She had downloaded an app, which was full of tourist information, locations and things to do locally. It linked with Google Maps so we could pinpoint our exact location and work out where we were heading. Her sunglasses were on top of her head, holding her glossy blonde hair back as she focused on the map. Not an ounce of sweat or glimpse of red on her face. *Lucky sod.*

"Wherever you like. It's only four o'clock so not time to eat yet."

I was hoping she would suggest going for gelato or a coffee, and sitting outside a coffee shop. Something nice, easy, relaxed and in the shade. There was plenty of time to do tourist stuff, but for today it would be nice to stay near the hotel and get used to the heat.

"Ooh! Let's walk to the Colosseum! It's only a mile away!"

A mile, in this heat? I will have burned off my pizza before I've even eaten it if we walk over there. I hope I don't get grumpy. Heat and hunger can be a dangerous combination.

"Let's do it." I smiled, determined to make it an amazing holiday for her.

Luckily, being from Yorkshire, we were used to cobbled roads trying to trip us up. I had no idea where we were going, but I trusted Sarah's navigational skills, even if we were in a foreign country and relying solely on an app. Not quite like the Ancient Romans did.

"Have you seen this?" she asked. "Look at the walls."

They were centuries old and looked like a strong gust of wind could blow them down, however, they had managed to survive this long. Maybe the Romans could consider invading England again and fixing our roads and walls. I'm sure no one would complain.

"Yeah, very old." I was not sure how one was supposed to compliment a wall. "Very... bricky?" Although these weren't bricks. They were made from stone. I have no idea how to entertain my history-loving friend.

"No, look!" This time she pointed. Carved into the wall was a cross. A crucifix. It was very worn, hard to see, but clear enough to make out once you'd spotted it. "I wonder if there is an old church nearby that we could look at."

"It's a very religious city. I'll bet there are more churches than coffee shops."

The sun was hitting my shoulders now, and I was beginning to feel the burn, even through my factor thirty suncream.

We knew we were heading to the centre of Rome, as the further we walked, the busier the streets became. Suddenly, we were walking amongst a crowd of people, which felt quite overwhelming. Sarah walked ahead, with her hand behind her back for me to hold, so we wouldn't lose each other. We had been warned by friends to keep our bags close to us and away from pickpockets, which were apparently rife in the city.

We decided to take a right down a quiet and narrow lane for a bit of breathing space. There was a tall building to one side of us, which had small shops on the ground floor and what must have been four floors of apartments above it, with shutters on all the windows. I was not sure what the old building on the other side was, though. Sarah had put her phone away now, for fear of it being snatched, so she wasn't too sure where we were either.

"I wonder what this old building is." I didn't respond. I could feel myself getting grumpy. The heat. The sweat. The hunger. The feel of hard stone beneath my flimsy sandals. I needed to find somewhere to sit with a cold drink.

Sarah seemed to pick up on my deteriorating mood. Luckily, she knew how to handle such a tricky and delicate situation.

"Let's walk around that way to see what it is, and then we can head for food."

It sounded like something you would say to a whining child to stop them from moaning, but it worked. I would be finally getting my Italian pizza, cooked by an Italian chef in the heart of Italy, and hopefully a bucket of ice for my feet to sit in.

We followed the path to the end of the road and rejoined

the crowd, following them like sheep to the front of the building. And... wow. This was not just any old building.

The enormous roof was being held up by rows and rows of pillars. I couldn't make out the wording that was carved on the front of the building, but it didn't stop me attempting to read it out loud. There were hundreds of people standing in and around the pillars, taking photos, touching them, leaning against them, sitting on the floor next to them. All in different poses for selfies, alone and with friends. *The Pantheon was something else.*

"Well," Sarah said. "Wow."

CHAPTER TWO

"How much?" I exclaimed.

We had managed to pull ourselves away from the Pantheon, through the crowds. There was a gelato stand not far from where we were, and I was busy reading the menu board.

"Why is it so expensive?" Sarah whispered.

"I don't know, but I'm not paying that much for a bottle of water," I said, not as quietly as Sarah. Hot, hungry me could not be silenced. "It's bloody mental!"

It was going to cost nearly fifty euros for two bottles of water and a scoop of gelato each. We'd agreed not to skimp on this trip, but I would not paying those kinds of prices, even if I was beginning to feel dehydrated. Prices were often higher in capital cities in the tourism hotspots, but we weren't expecting this.

"Come on, there must be a little shop or something around here where it is a lot cheaper."

"Mi scusi, ladies?" a deep voice said from behind us.

We turned to see who was talking to us. If they *were* even talking to us. There were so many people around us that we could have been mistaken. Then he stepped forward. I don't know how he was able to cope in his suit with this heat, but there was not an ounce of sweat on him. His long, black hair was swept back, and he had beautiful skin. His hair was beautiful. *He* was beautiful.

"I'm so sorry, ladies," he said in very good English. "Please, come."

He gestured for us to follow him away from the crowd.

"Is it safe?" I asked Sarah, whose lower lip was almost touching the floor.

"If he wants to kidnap me, he can. Come on."

She grabbed my hand and pulled me through the crowd to follow the mysterious Italian man. He did not lead us down an abandoned alley. Instead, he took us away from the hoard of people, into a more open area closer to the Pantheon.

"I'm sorry, I can see you are on holiday so I no bother you for long, but my advice? Don't buy from 'ere." He pointed to the gelato stand where we had just been, and to the other vendors scattered around. "You should buy from less busy place. Outside the main part of the city. Is cheaper. These prices? Crazy."

"Ah, right," I said. Sarah was in a trance, listening to him speak. "Thank you. It's so nice of you to tell us. We'll find somewhere else."

"How long you been in Rome?" he asked.

"We only arrived this afternoon. We were just going to have a walk before finding somewhere to eat. Where would you recommend?"

"You will find lots of places hidden in the old roads. If there are tourists? Keep walking. If there are Italians? You know is a good place." He had a great smile. His white teeth stood out against his olive skin.

"Thank you." Sarah had finally woken up from her man-coma. "Are you from Rome?"

"No, I am from Foggia, a little bit south of 'ere. I now live in Rome, for work."

"Ah, that sounds wonderful. What a beautiful place to live."

They were staring deeply into each other's eyes. A subtle smile, and the odd twinkle, definitely a connection. All thoughts of Max The Wanker and the abandoned wedding had clearly been pushed well out of Sarah's mind, thanks to our new Italian friend.

"My name is Alessandro." He held out his hand, to shake ours in turn.

"I'm Sarah, and this is Jenny."

"It is nice to meet you, ladies. But I must apologise. I must leave. Maybe we will see each other again, yes?"

"Yes. That would be great, yes. Jenny?" Sarah looked at me.

"Absolutely." This was the first time in a long time that any smile on her face had seemed genuine. Until now, any man who'd dared to speak to her in the past three months had been kindly told to eff off. "We're here for a few days so, definitely."

"Good, good." He fumbled around in his pocket and pulled out a card. "This is my number. We can meet for a drink, or something." I could almost feel the electricity as his hand touched Sarah's and she took the card from him. She ran her other hand through her hair, brushing a strand of it behind her ear. She wasn't even blushing. If that were me, I would be as red as a pepperoni.

"I'll let you know what we're doing, and then we can arrange something."

"That sounds wonderful. *Grazie.*" He stepped back, ready to walk away from us, having one final glance at Sarah. "*Ciao*, ladies."

"Yes, *ciao*."

~

"That accent though. Did you hear how he said his name?" Sarah had been busy swooning over her new Italian friend throughout our entire meal. We followed Alessandro's advice and found a restaurant near our hotel that was filled with locals. And he was right. The food was perfecto as well as cheapo.

"I did." I picked up another slice of pizza. I was having a foodgasm, and hardly even listening to what she was saying.

"*Alessandro.* Oh, how his tongue rolled when he said it. Alessandrrro. Imagine what else that tongue could do."

"Well," I said, with a mouthful of melted cheesy goodness. "We're here for a little while longer. Plenty of time to find out. My God, this is good pizza."

"Do you think we should meet up with him? Is that a good idea? No, we can't. I can't. Can I? No, no, I can't."

"Why not?" I asked, taking another huge bite.

"Because it's our holiday. A girly holiday. Not a man-meeting holiday."

"Neither was Zante, and we both know how that turned out." I cringed at the memory, and about the awkwardness of Sarah's parents picking us up from the airport just thirty-six hours after they had dropped us off. They had kindly agreed not to call my mother and allowed me to hide at their house for the remainder of the week so she never had to know of my shame.

"That was different! We were twenty-one. Single girls in their twenties can get away with that kind of stuff. I'm thirty-one now. It's time to be mature. Sensible. One must refrain from climbing on top of sexy Italian men."

"What are you talking about? You can do whatever you want."

She leaned back in her chair and swirled her fork in her spaghetti, but not lifting any to her mouth to eat.

I tried to ignore the giant, sparkly pink elephant in the room, but it was difficult not to work out what was on her mind in that moment. Max The Wanker's girlfriend Ellie was in her twenties. Twenty-three, to be exact.

"Age has nothing to do with it."

"You say that, but you'll notice it from now on. Everywhere you go, there'll be a bunch of twenty-year-old girls having more fun than you. They go around in groups, hunting. You're okay, you have a man who adores you. I've got a battle on my hands now, if I ever want to meet someone."

"Well, Alessandro didn't seem to notice any of the twenty-year-olds standing around us in their miniskirts. It was *us* he pulled from the crowd, and he only had eyes for you. Text him if you want. We can meet him tomorrow evening. I don't mind."

"Are you sure? I don't want you feeling like a gooseberry."

"I'll be fine. Just tell him to meet us somewhere near the hotel, so I can sneak back if I want to. It'll give me an excuse to give Zack a call." *And try out phone sex.*

"Okay, but I'll text him in the morning. I don't want to seem too eager."

The sun was setting. It was still humid outside, but this place had air conditioning, so we were nice and cool inside. Sarah took her last mouthful of pasta, and I crunched down on the pizza crust, which was too delicious to leave on the plate. I was full. The antipasti, the salads, the bread, and finally the pizza.

"Your meal is good, *si?*" Our waiter, Matteo, returned. He was the only English-speaking waiter at the restaurant. He was funny, although it was sometimes difficult to understand him. Or to get him to understand us.

"*Si,* yes, it was perfect, thank you."

"You like tiramisu?" he asked, full of hope.

"Oh no, thank you. We're too full."

"You no like tiramisu?" He pretended to get upset and

wiped a fake tear from his eye. "My nonna make it. You make-a me sad."

I laughed. "We do like tiramisu. We're just too full." We both rubbed our bellies for effect. Hoping he would understand.

"You like tiramisu?"

"Yes!" we both said together.

"Okay, okay, you insist then I bring." He smiled in victory, giving me a wink.

"We will need to do a lot of walking tomorrow to burn all of this off," I said to Sarah as Matteo removed our collection of empty plates from the table.

"That won't be a problem, I'm sure!" she pulled out her phone and opened up the Rome app. "Look where we can go!"

CHAPTER THREE

I stared at the food Leonardo had brought us for breakfast. He kindly took it out to the balcony, insisting we sat outside to eat at our little shaded table. He had brought us a selection of pastries, fruit, bread and jam. Maria followed with our coffees. She seemed less angry this morning. She even managed to give us a smile, which was surprising as we were still in our pyjamas.

"I know we're full from last night, but this looks so good. And not a biscotti in sight." I picked up one of the bread rolls and cut into it, smothering it in butter and Maria's homemade jam.

"How can you eat more bread after all that last night?" Sarah asked, as she picked up a banana. "We will be overdosing on carbs. I'll have some grapes, but I just don't think I can manage anything else right now."

"You might as well eat and fill up now whilst you can. If we're out walking in the touristy places then food will cost a fortune. I doubt we'll come across any more Alessandros willing to guide us in the right direction." I bit into the bread. It was so soft, almost like candyfloss the way it melted in my mouth. "Why don't we turn the rest of these bread rolls into jam sandwiches and take them out with us to have later? We can eat properly tonight."

We decided to have the pastries for breakfast before making a mini picnic to take with us. We wrapped the sandwiches in a tea towel Leonardo had left. It was still early, but the sun was now up and shining down the narrow road and onto our balcony. We watched as the locals set about their days, as we sat back in our chairs with our feet up on the railings. Sarah and I had been on a lot of holidays together, but so far, this was the most grown-up one to date. We were hangover-free and up early enough for breakfast. How very mature of us.

"So, where shall we go today?" I asked. We'd decided not to make an itinerary for this trip, or prebook anything, deciding that it would put too much pressure on us to make sure we got to certain places on time. We had an idea about the places we wanted to visit, but thought we would wing it each day.

"How about we walk in the direction of the Trevi Fountain?" She picked up her phone.

"Sounds good, but how far is it?" I hid my trepidation behind another sip of cappuccino.

"Just a little further on than the Pantheon, so not too far." She studied the map on the app. "Ooh! We can do a circle and check out the Colosseum on the way back, seeing as we didn't make it there yesterday. That will fill our day."

"Let's do it. I might have to wear my trainers today though." I massaged the heel of my left foot, which had been feeling tender, hoping I wouldn't end up with a blister. Those sandals were a bad idea yesterday.

"I thought that too. You'd think we'd be used to walking, being from Yorkshire."

I stood up and picked up some plates to take back inside. "I'll have a quick shower, and you can text Alessandro."

"I can't text him now, it's far too early."

"I'm sure he'll be awake. He was dressed all businessman-like when we saw him, so he'll likely be on his way to work. Message him. Say exactly what we discussed last night. 'Hello, this is Sarah from yesterday. Thank you for the advice on where to eat. How about meeting for a drink tonight? X'. Something basic and not too pushy."

She hesitated, holding her phone in her hand. The more she thought about it, I knew the less likely it was that the message would get sent.

"Don't overthink this. You're not proposing anything serious. It is just a drink. A. Harmless. Drink."

I left her with her thoughts and grabbed my phone on the way to the bathroom. There was a message waiting for me from Zack.

> Good morning, baby, I hope you slept okay and weren't too warm. Bing slept on my chest and wasn't budging, no matter how much I tried to move. I was roasting. He must be missing you. As am I. What are your plans today? Xxx

I was still wearing my giddy schoolgirl grin as I got in the shower after sending him a reply with our plans. This was a very refreshing, mature relationship. I didn't need to worry about what Zack was up to. I doubted he would be distracted by a twenty-something.

> Good morning! I miss you too. More exploring on the agenda today. I might need to schedule a foot massage when I'm home, if you can fit me in... Xxx

> I can always fit you in, I'll be on hand for all of your needs when you get back. Enjoy your day :) Xxx

When Sarah and I were finally ready, we set off walking in our comfy trainers. Once again, Sarah's hair was elegantly flowing in the light breeze, slipping off her shoulders as she walked, and mine was already starting to stick to me. I knew wearing it down would be a bad idea, so I pulled the spare bobble off my wrist, quickly tied it all back into a makeshift bun, and pulled out my handheld fan to waft my neck.

"Has Alessandro replied yet?"

"No, not yet. He probably won't. I bet he was just being nice to the two lost tourists last night. He'll do it all the time. He won't have been serious about meeting up."

"Of course he was being serious. Why else would he give you a card with his phone number on it? He'll reply." I wasn't used to seeing Sarah lacking in confidence and being so down on herself. This wasn't her, and it was difficult to witness. "Sarah." I held out my arm to get her to stop walking and turn to face me. It was pep-talk time. "You've been through one of the worst years ever. First, Max The Wanker had an affair and subsequently ended your engagement. Then, he fucked up the mortgage payments so you had to move out of your dream home with very little notice. You *deserve* to have some fun. You *deserve* to have a hot Italian guy flirt with you and take you out for drinks. He *will* reply, and tonight you are going to take back your happiness. It's been gone for too long, and I miss my friend, Sarah. She has got to make her comeback."

A small tear escaped her eye, making its way down her cheek. She wiped it away and managed a smile.

"Yes, you're right. I'm sorry. I've sulked and moped about all this for long enough. It's time to move on and stop feeling sorry for myself."

"Yes, it is. And don't say sorry. I'm always here if you need to talk, but you need to get back on the horse. Or mount a stallion. Now, let's get to the fountain. My feet aren't aching yet, so you've got plenty of time before I start moaning at you."

I linked my arm in hers, and we carried on with our journey, smiles on our faces.

~

"*What do you mean you have to move?*" I asked Sarah, as she frantically cried down the phone to me.

"*Max hasn't been paying the mortgage.*" She took a deep breath. "*And he's had all his mail redirected to his new place, so I haven't known about any of this until now.*"

"*But you've been paying your share, haven't you? Can't they take that into account?*"

"*The payments come out of his bank account. I've been transferring my share to him so payments can be made, but he hasn't been passing them on. Just pocketing my money. I'm screwed.*"

"*What a wanker! What does your letter say?*"

"*That I have thirty-one days to vacate. On my thirty-first birthday I get thirty-one days to vacate, before they seek possession and send the bailiffs. What am I going to do?*"

"*Don't you have any rights? You kept to your share of the payments, you have proof, it's not your fault he stole your money.*"

"*Apparently there's not a lot I can do. I called them this morning. They don't care about personal disputes. They just want paying, or they repossess the house. There's no way I can pay all this. I wouldn't even be able to afford to buy him out to take it on myself.*"

"*What an absolute cockwomble!*" I was filled with so much rage I could have burst into tears myself, but I had to be strong for my friend.

"I'm going to be homeless!" she cried. "How? How could any of this have happened?"

"No, you're not going to be homeless. No one would ever let that happen. You can stay with me. I have plenty of room. I can clear out the spare room for you, there's already a bed in there. Zack will help bring your things across. You can stay for as long as you need to. We'll sort this out together."

"Oh, thank you." She struggled to talk through the tears. "I can't believe it. I'm losing my home. First, my fiancé, and now my dream home. What else can that guy do to me?"

The Trevi Fountain was, as the Italians would say, 'amaze-a-balls-a'. No other words could adequately describe it. We stood in silence for what felt like hours and hours, just taking in all the detail.

"Well," Sarah said. "Now *that's* a fountain. Trafalgar Square, eat your heart out."

"It sure is."

Above the sea of heads were smartphones on selfie sticks, like balloons on a string floating above us. Hundreds of them. No one seemed to be taking in the sight with their own eyes, they were just looking through the cameras on their phones. Well, the younger lot were. The older generations were enjoying it, like us. Oh my God, are we now classed as the older generation? Hell, no. I pulled out my own phone and started snapping away, taking photos of the fountain and the odd selfie, some of Sarah and me, and then Sarah on her own. Then I saw it.

Over Sarah's shoulder, on the other side of the fountain, I could see a man down on one knee with a ring in his hand, holding it up to a very emotional and happy woman in her twenties. *Shit.* Sarah did *not* need to be seeing these levels of romance. This holiday was supposed to make her forget that it was supposed to be her wedding week. We had to get moving. She could not see this.

I returned my glance to Sarah to suggest we should start our walk to the next location, when I saw the huge, beaming smile on her face. She was looking at her phone too, but not through the camera.

"Alessandro has replied," she said. "He's going to meet us later."

By the time we got back to our hotel, my feet were throbbing. Even in my brand-new memory-foam Skechers, my feet were defeated. We must have walked at least ten miles in circles, going back and forth to see things we had missed. I couldn't complain really, Rome was spectacular. And once Sarah received that text from Alessandro, she'd been practically bouncing from place to place. I had struggled to keep up with her.

"We can try the bus tomorrow, if you like?" Sarah watched me cringing as I carefully removed my trainers and gently peeled my socks off. "It might help our feet to recover."

"Definitely, ahh." A blister on my little toe had popped, and the sock felt like it had been cemented to it. "Oh, that stings."

It had just turned five o'clock. We had two hours to go before we were meeting Alessandro at the bistro down the street. That meant I had two hours to soak my feet in ice-cold water in the hope that they would forgive me. I have put them through some tough times in my life, but this was their limit.

"Are you having another shower?" Sarah asked.

"I think I will." Rome in June was proving to be a hot one.

Especially when walking around as much as we had been. "Shall I go first?"

"Yes, I'll try to get online and book tickets to the Colosseum."

We had already made it to the Colosseum earlier that afternoon, hoping to get in, but we had never seen queues like it. The worst queue I had ever witnessed until then was the day the final Harry Potter book was released for sale in Waterstones, but this was unbelievable. There was no way in hell we would have made it inside before it closed. And with the sun belting down on us, it wouldn't have taken long for us to melt. We had heard an older couple in the queue arguing with each other because the wife had apparently instructed the husband to book the tickets online, but the husband didn't, because he insisted she had not told him to do anything of the sort. The husband then got an earful, before loudly asking a passing tour guide if the lions were still in the pits so he could throw his wife in. They both looked miserable in each other's company. We sat on a wall in some shade and took out our jam sandwiches to eat whilst watching the drama unfold.

Before I stood up from the bed, taking deep breaths in anticipation of the pain that was sure to shoot through my feet as soon as I placed them on the floor, I had a quick glance to the coffee table.

"Is that new biscotti?"

On a white plate, with gold paint intricately decorating the edges, was some chocolate biscotti.

"That woman is a biscotti baking machine!" Sarah said, picking one up and taking a bite. "Wow, these ones are good."

"Anything made of chocolate is good." I hobbled to the table and helped myself to one. Sarah was right. The last batch had barely been touched, as they were rock hard and had too many almonds in them. I suspected these ones wouldn't last the night.

"Right, I won't be long in the shower. Then you can start glamming yourself up." I winked at my nervous friend and took my hot, swollen feet to the bathroom, feeling instant relief as I stepped onto the cold marble floor.

~

"I have heard of Halifax." Alessandro was leaning across the table, gazing at Sarah. "I visited London some years ago and think I saw Halifax."

"Oh, Halifax isn't in London," Sarah said.

"Hmm, I thought I saw a sign, with a big blue cross." He held his arms in front of him to form an 'X' shape.

"Ah, I think you mean the bank. There will be a lot of Halifax banks in London. *Our* Halifax is a town in Yorkshire, up in the north of England."

"Okay, okay." He seemed embarrassed. "I am sorry, my mistake. In that case, I have not seen Halifax."

"That's okay," Sarah said. "It's an easy mistake to make." She pointed at me. "This one thought Pisa was down the road from here." They both laughed and were staring into each other's eyes like two teenagers scared to admit they fancied each other.

Even though I had my own man at home, I could still appreciate how gorgeous this man was. He must have been in his thirties, like us. He dressed very smartly and seemed quite well off. I tried to pay for a round of drinks for us, but he would not allow it. I liked him even more after that.

Conversation between him and Sarah seemed easy, despite the slight language barrier. He spoke really good English. I didn't actually mind that I was playing the gooseberry this evening. Sarah lost her twinkle after Max The Wanker broke her heart, but this evening her eyes were shining again. I could feel her coming back to me. It was great to witness. Apparently, the cure to a broken heart was a sexy Italian man.

As happy as I had been to witness Sarah's comeback, I realised it was getting quite late, and I wanted to phone Zack for a quick chat. I was about to make my excuses and leave, when Alessandro stood up.

"I will be back, *mi scusi*, ladies."

He wandered to the back of the bistro to the gents' toilets.

"Jen, how's my hair? Do I have anything in my teeth? Is my make-up okay?"

"You look gross. Total train wreck."

She slapped my leg. "I'm being serious! He is so yummy, and I feel like a sweaty, horrible slob. It's so humid here."

"Sarah, you look fabulous. Your hair is glossy and enviably perfect, despite the humidity. Your make-up hasn't smudged, and he seems so besotted with you. He hasn't taken his eyes off you. Enjoy it."

"Okay, okay. I just feel so *awkward* chatting and flirting with a guy. I've not done this for years. I feel so out of practice. This is the first guy since, you know who, that I haven't wanted to kill."

"Well, you're doing amazing for someone who up until now has wished death on anyone with a penis. Including Santa."

"That pervert deserved what he got."

I don't think I will ever forget the image of horrified children as Sarah threw eggnog in the face of the poor Santa who was handing out candy canes and sharing sweet words of Christmas cheer last December. '*And here is one for the pretty lady. Merry Christmas!*' is all he'd said as he had handed some candy to Sarah with a cheery smile. One eggnog shower later and we were both escorted out of the shopping centre by security. We have not been back since.

"Well, anyway, you're doing great this evening. I was single for years and never managed to stay as calm and collected as you are when I was around someone I fancied."

Alessandro appeared back at our table.

"More espresso, ladies? I can order some if you like?" he asked.

"Oh, no thanks. I think I'll go back to the hotel, actually." I looked at Sarah. "I can phone Zack and say goodnight. Is that okay?"

"Yes, sure, that's fine."

"I will make sure Sarah get back safely, do not worry," Alessandro said.

Seeing as the hotel was approximately twenty metres away, I was sure she would be fine.

"Okay, thank you so much again for the drinks." Alessandro leaned in and did the European 'kiss on each cheek' thing. "I'll see you back at the hotel," I said to Sarah, giving her a sly wink before leaving.

I walked into the hotel entrance and was met by Maria. She must have been on the wine. Her cheeks were rosy and she seemed very happy to see me, pulling me in for my second 'kiss on each cheek' of the day. She held onto my hands as she was speaking to me, but I had no idea what she was saying. All I could make out was, *'Bella ragazza inglese!'* which I assumed meant 'I made you more biscotti'.

"I'm going to bed, Maria. Very sleepy."

"Ah, *si, si,* go sleep." She smiled at me. "I bring more biscotti tomorrow."

"Oh, we would love more of the chocolate biscotti please. They're our favourite."

"Chocolate?" The grip on my hands tightened.

"Yes, the ones you left for us this afternoon. There aren't many left, I'm afraid. We couldn't help ourselves."

Her pink cheeks turned into furious-red cheeks. She still

had hold of my hands and the grip was almost unbearable. I feared they would be crushed in her Hulk-like grip. Just at that moment, a sheepish Leonardo appeared, holding a glass of red wine.

"*Biscotti al cioccolato?*" she said to him, releasing her hold of my poor hands. "*Idiota!*"

And then, World War Three was declared right in the lobby. Italy against Italy. Traditional biscotti against rebellious chocolate biscotti. Maria was winning the battle, for sure. I felt very awkward, as Maria's argument was very animated, with a hand gesture in my direction for every angry word. Italians seemed to have their own sign language for getting a point across. Maria didn't need to bother, though. Her anger was palpable.

Maria finally stormed out of the room and into the kitchen, where more banging and cluttering followed. Leonardo looked at me unphased, and smiled.

"I am sorry, Maria no like chocolate biscotti. I make them for English lady guests. They are popular. But Maria no like it. She, ah, she want to make traditional."

"I'm so sorry if I've got you into trouble!" I was mortified and scared for him.

"It no bother." He smiled. "I bring you more in the morning." He winked, and turned to go through a different door, far away from Maria. I pulled my phone out of my bag and typed a message to Sarah.

> Don't rush back. Maria is on the rampage and I got Leonardo in trouble! Whatever you do, don't bring up the chocolate biscotti with her!!! I'll explain later. Enjoy the rest of your evening. Have fun! 😔 Xxx

Getting back to the safety of the room was a relief. It was

peaceful, away from the noise of Maria's wrath, and it was also cool thanks to the air conditioning. I slipped off my sandals and curled up on the small couch whilst scrolling for Zack's number in my phone.

"Hey you." His voice was like music to my ears. "Everything okay?"

"Hey! Yes, it's all good here. Just thought I'd check in. Are you all right? Are you free for a chat?"

"Yeah, I've just got to yours to let Bing in and give him some food."

"How's he doing?"

"He's great, he's barely left me alone since I walked in. I've just been out for tea with my mum and dad. All they did was talk about you. They can't wait to meet you. I think they like you already."

I was looking forward to meeting them. They lived in Spain for most of the year, but had come home for a couple of months to see family and friends, and I suspected to escape the southern Spanish heat. English summers are known for being cold and dreary, after all.

"Unluckily for you, that means you can't dump me for a hot young blonde."

"I know. Dammit. Had my eye on one, too."

"Well, my hot blonde bombshell is currently out having drinks with her new Italian boyfriend, so looks like you're stuck with me for a bit right now."

"Sarah is out with a guy?" His tone had changed. "On her own? Is that safe?"

"Yes. She's a grown-up now so she doesn't need minding."

"Did you say you were back at the hotel? I'd hate to think you were out on your own, you never know what could happen."

"Zack, honestly, it's fine. She will be fine. He's a nice guy and it's making her happy. Which is what this holiday is all about."

"If you're sure."

"I am. Anyway, the bistro they're at is literally across the road. If I lean far enough over the balcony, I'll be able to see them staring into each other's eyes feeding amaretto to each other.

"If you say so."

If this was Zack's attitude to a mature, grown-up date in a foreign country, then it would be best he never heard about our holiday to Zante all those years ago. He would *not* approve. Some things were best kept secret.

"So, tell me more about dinner with your parents? What's new with them?"

"Not much. Same old, same old. They asked about you, about work, more about you. They want me to organise a meal out with us and them when you get back if that's okay?"

"Of course it is. I can't wait to meet them. We can sort it out next week."

"Good. I'll let them know. Anyway, why are we talking on the phone as if it's the nineties? Have you got wifi there? Call me on WhatsApp video, I want a sneak peek of those white bits."

CHAPTER FOUR

Leonardo brought us our breakfast at exactly seven thirty the next morning, smiling as always. I was glad he had survived the night unscathed. On the tray, along with our coffees, bread, fruit and pastries, was another plate covered with a napkin. He placed the tray down on the table, and winked at me with a cheeky grin, putting his finger over his lips.

When he was gone, and the door was firmly shut, I pulled back the napkin and saw half a dozen chocolate biscotti. I giggled and shook my head at his daredevil activities. When Sarah had got back the night before, I'd explained 'biscotti-gate' to her and that we would be avoiding Maria as much as possible between now and when it was time to go home.

I poured us both some coffee and had a nibble of the biscotti before preparing our little picnic for the day. There was a hint of coffee mixed in with the chocolate flavour this time. I needed to take some of these home with me. I'd need to ask Leonardo for the recipe. I could bake a batch and impress my mother with my new European culinary skills.

Sarah emerged from the bathroom, smiling to herself.

"Still smiling from last night? Must have been a good one."

"Alessandro has just texted me, wishing me a good day. That's all." She slid her phone into her back pocket.

"Are you seeing him again?"

"I think he wants to take me out for dinner tomorrow night. He's checking his work schedule... but it will be our last night here so I'm not sure I should. It should be us girls doing something special."

"*We* can go for dinner anytime we want to back home. If you want to see him, go and see him."

"I'll see." She picked up a biscotti and dipped it in her coffee. "Oh, that reminds me." She put her drink and biscuit down and went over to her bag, pulling out some pieces of paper. "He gave me these bus tickets."

"Okay, I suppose flowers and chocolates are rather old school."

"I told him we were going to attempt the buses to get around today, and he said you need to buy tickets before you get on the bus, or you can get fined. He buys loads in advance so he's never short of one. He just said to make sure we get them validated on the buses, or something along those lines, and we'll be fine. Didn't sound too complicated when he explained it so it should be easy enough."

"Oh, great stuff. Well, I don't fancy spending the night in an Italian police cell, or walking any further on my poor sore feet. Keep those tickets safe in your bag." My feet, although all right in appearance, were feeling very tender.

"Did you ask him which bus we need to get to the Colosseum?"

"Yes, I wrote it all down in my phone. I've got the entry tickets downloaded to my phone too – and I'm fully charged." She had a little giddy spring in her step. "Let's eat quickly, I booked our entry time for nine thirty and we need to be at the ticket desk thirty minutes before that, according to the app."

I picked up another biscotti.

"Eat something proper for breakfast, or you won't have any energy. I imagine we'll be wandering around the colosseum for ages. Especially if it's busy and we're in a crowd of people."

"Yes, Mum." I picked up another biscotti and shoved it into my bag along with the sandwiches.

Sarah, being the more sensible of us that morning, picked up the pastries and wrapped them in tissue, putting them in her bag for us too. Her phone buzzed again. She pulled it out of her pocket to read the message. Judging by the grin on her face, it was a good one.

"It's Alessandro. He can't do tomorrow after all, but was wondering if I want to have dinner with him tonight instead." She bit her bottom lip and sat down on the bed. "What do I say?"

"You say yes!"

"Are you sure you don't mind? It is supposed to be our girly getaway. I feel awful abandoning you."

"Well, why don't you suggest that we all eat together? Then I can come back here with an excuse of being tired or something."

"No, I'll tell him that you and I are eating together, but we can meet for drinks afterwards."

"That sounds perfect. A good compromise."

She made her arrangements with her Italian man-friend and then we finished getting ready for our outing and set off to find a bus stop. Sarah had all the information on where we were going, so I was just following her. Her mood had definitely lifted since arriving here. Max The Wanker had done a good job at breaking her spirit.

❧

I'd arrived home from work later than normal. I had been stuck with a customer who just wouldn't stop complaining about everything. Eventually, Samantha had stepped in to finish the meeting for me so I could leave, as the caretaker had arrived to start locking up the building. My drive home was no better. I hit every set of roadworks possible on the way. It was as though all the temporary traffic lights saw me coming and switched to red. Why do they all come at once?

"Sorry I'm late!" I called to Sarah. She had been staying at my house for the previous three weeks since being forced to leave her home. I had been working overtime, trying to keep her spirits up as much as possible. It was a big change for her, downsizing from her three-bedroom detached house and into my spare room. We'd had an amazing Christmas, despite the Santa incident, and we threw a New Year's Eve party together. It was just like when we were living together at university. "How about fish and chips for tea? I can nip back out." I hung my coat up in the hallway, and walked into the living room, but she wasn't there. "Sarah? Are you in?" I was sure I'd seen her car parked on the road.

I walked into the kitchen, but she wasn't there either.

"Hello?" I called out again.

"Here." A muffled voice came from upstairs.

My first thought was about the house she was trying to buy. She had found a bungalow not far from here that she loved. It was the perfect size for her, affordable thanks to the bank of Mum and Dad, plus the small amount of equity she had been paid from the sale of the old house. I hoped her offer hadn't been declined. That was not the kind of news she needed.

"Where are you?" I walked up the stairs and into the spare room. She was sitting at the end of the bed. Her tear-stained face was red and blotchy. "What's happened? Is it the house?" I sat down next to her and put my arms around her, but she didn't say

anything. She just stared at the wall. "Sarah, talk to me. What's happened?"

"It's not the house."

"Then what is it?" I was wracking my brain, wondering if she had told me that her elderly grandma was ill, or if it was that time of the month.

"Max."

"What has that wanker done now?"

"She's pregnant."

"Who's pregnant?"

"The child bride he left me for. He's got her pregnant. Stupid, fertile child."

Ah. Max's twenty-three-year-old girlfriend was knocked up. Damn.

She handed me her phone, which had Facebook open. A mutual 'friend' had shared Max's post announcing the news, with a photo of the happy couple holding a sonogram picture together.

"Oh, I see."

"He told me he didn't want children. Not for years, anyway. 'They tie you down,' he always said. Didn't want them interrupting his precious career, so I was the moron who had the implant all those years to keep him happy. I wanted kids. I couldn't wait to have kids. I put it on hold for him and his fucking job, which he's packed in now, apparently. He's not even moving to Canada anymore. They're staying here to raise their mutant baby and I am just single, thirty, childless and homeless."

How can a man be so determined to do one thing and live a certain way, and then so easily change his mind as soon as he gets into a new relationship?

"Look, you can't think about that now." I put her phone out of reach. "Firstly, you will never be homeless. Too many of us love you too much to let that happen. And don't get worked up over what he's doing. I told you at the start of this break-up that things will likely get worse before they start to get better, but they will get better. You'll see." I pulled some clean tissue from my pocket and wiped the tears from her face.

"Losing the home that I worked so hard for was supposed to be the worst part of all this. That should have been it. Things were supposed to be on the up by now. I'm this close to getting a new house. A house all of my own. I even got that promotion at work last week. Karma seemed to be working in my favour. And then it's two steps forward and ten steps backwards." She scrunched up the tissues which had been clenched in her hands, and threw them at the bin, missing.

"Hey, you have taken a hundred steps forward over the last few months. Look at you! You're going to own your own house, that's huge! Plus, you've just been promoted with a huge pay rise. That's amazing! Yes, you want kids, but can you imagine if you'd had them with that wanker? He still would have betrayed you. You'd now be a single mum, sharing a bed with a baby in my spare room. And the best news is, now he's no longer your problem."

She sighed, so I continued.

"You shouldn't be upset that he's going to be a dad, you should be sad because that poor child will be raised by them on that awful estate. And it doesn't matter how young she is, if she can live with herself, knowing how he is treating you, then it says a lot about her. They're welcome to each other."

She managed a little laugh.

"Look at the bigger picture. Look at what is going on in your life at the moment. That should be your main focus. We need to plan on decorating your new house when you get the keys, shopping for furniture and knick-knacks. But most importantly..." I had a serious look on my face and waited until she took notice, wondering what I was going to say. "Most *importantly…" I brushed a strand of her hair behind her ear. "What do you want from the chippy, because I am bloody starving?"*

~

I am pleased to report that the Italian buses felt a lot sturdier and safer than the taxi ride we had experienced from the airport. The first bus we got on was packed full of people, but we managed to find two seats together at the back. It was warm and sticky with all the bodies exuding heat around us, so I pulled out my trusty fan whilst Sarah seemed to be engrossed in something on her phone.

"Don't forget, you're the map," I reminded her. "I don't know where we're getting off. Keep your head up."

"That's what I'm doing." She showed me her phone. "The blue dot is where we need to get off. Anywhere near there will do."

"Great. Although it's so bloody warm in here it might have been cooler if we'd walked."

"Don't say that now, we have all these tickets to use up."

It took only five more minutes to arrive at our destination. We pushed our way through the sweaty folk crowded onto the bus, and finally made it out into the fresh air. We were in the shade and a welcome breeze blew under our arms, relieving us of some of the early morning heat.

We had exited the bus onto one of the older, less touristy streets of Rome, so we were glad when we found a small shop that did not charge us the earth for a bottle of water. We grabbed one each, and after a difficult attempt at a conversation with the Italian owner, he convinced us to buy a hat each too.

"No roof!" he managed to say, talking about the Colosseum

after we'd double-checked with him that we were heading in the right direction. "The sun, on your head? Hot. Bad."

Two bottles of water, two hats and a handheld fan for Sarah later, we were ready. We thought he had just conned us into spending more money, and then we saw the Colosseum. He was right. There was no sign of shade anywhere, so we would have had the sun beating down on us for our entire visit.

We had ten minutes until we needed to be at the ticket counter, so we stood and stared at the impressive structure. I am not a fan of history, it never interested me at all in school, but even I could appreciate this sight. It took our breath away. Once again, there was a wave of cameras and selfie sticks around us. Even though it was early, there was a huge queue of people wanting to get inside.

"And that is why we booked our tickets," Sarah said, pointing to the snaking queues. "Come on, let's head to the ticket counter. I want to see if there is a guidebook I can buy. Ooh, I wonder if that old married couple are still arguing."

"Hmm, maybe he locked her in the pits below and jetted off to a peaceful remote island."

"Ha, possibly. As long as they're not on the tour with us. Last thing we need is to hear someone else's marital problems."

My thoughts went back to Leonardo as we walked to the ticket counter. I wondered if he had ever been tempted to lock Maria in an ancient cell.

"Jenny, you would love my village," Alessandro said while we were having our drinks together that evening. "It is a small village, but everyone is like family. And they all want to feed you. So, if you want to go for a nice, simple walk, go at night so no one see you. Or else, you must eat *another* bowl of pasta."

Sarah and I had been laughing at his stories all evening. "That is why I leave to come here to the city. My health! You cannot say no to a nonna with food. She will do this," he pretended to hit the back of his head, "very angry if you say no."

"Well, tell me how to get there," I said with a laugh. "Food on demand? That sounds like my perfect holiday."

"If you love food, move to Italy. Everyone want to feed you."

"There's my life goal," I said. "I'll need to convince Zack to move with me, though. Oh bugger, what time is it?"

"It's almost nine o'clock."

"I said I'd call him at nine. I'll leave you guys to it, if that's okay?"

"We can walk you?" Alessandro stood up.

"No, no, it's fine. It's only down the road." I stood up and grabbed my bag. "Thank you so much for the drinks again, it's been great meeting you."

"You too, Jenny." He kissed both of my cheeks.

"I'll see you back at the hotel." I winked at Sarah before leaving the bar. Then I pulled my phone out of my bag and called Zack, so he could keep me company as I wandered back.

"Hello." I loved hearing his voice. I couldn't wait to see him.

"Hey, you."

"Hey, you too, not long now. It feels as though you've been gone for ages."

"I know, tell me about it. I can't wait to see you. Have you missed me?"

"You know I have. Being in your bed isn't the same without you here too. Bing is all right for company, but his services as a cat are limited." I was relieved that Zack had agreed to stay over some nights, so Bing wouldn't be alone for too long.

"Aw, Bing! I've missed him too."

"Why are you out of breath?"

"I'm on my way back to the hotel." I had a slight sprint to

my step. "We met Alessandro after dinner for drinks at the bar again. I've left Sarah with him. He's so funny. They're really getting on. You won't believe how much she's changed since meeting him."

"She likes him then?"

"Yes, I think so. They look good together, too. I think he is just what she needs to bring her out of her slump."

"I'm glad to hear it. Are you back at the hotel yet?"

"Just about, I'm walking up the steps now. Need to try and avoid Maria if I can. I don't want to start another matrimonial war. I don't think the Catholics favour divorce very much."

I opened the door slowly, and peeked in to check if it was safe to enter.

"There's no one here," I whispered. "I'll make a run for it up the stairs. Hang on."

I had just managed to close the door when Leonardo appeared.

"Oh, hi..." I began.

"Shh." He put his finger to his mouth and handed me a small package. "Put in your suitcase." He finished handing over the illicit goods and then quietly shuffled back through the kitchen door.

"What's going on? Are you okay?" Zack asked.

"Yeah, my new adopted grandad appeared, and has given me a small parcel."

"What's inside it?"

"I don't know for sure, but I have a sneaking suspicion." I sprinted up the stairs and made it into my room, almost dropping the phone while fishing about in my bag for the key. I sat down on the couch and put the parcel on the coffee table, along with my phone on loudspeaker. I unwrapped the thin cloth and there was a large batch of chocolate biscotti. "Ha! Amazing."

"What is it?"

"It's a load of chocolate biscotti. Bless him! Now you'll be able to try some, if I don't eat it all tonight. There is a lot of it, though, it might push my luggage allowance over the limit. I'll have to give Sarah half of it. Unless he has another batch for her too." I secretly hoped he did.

"So then, how much have you eaten on this trip? More or less than you'd expected?"

"More. Absolutely more. You won't recognise me. I've gained enough weight to throw the plane off balance."

"Well, I hope you will be sharing that biscotti with me. We can gain weight together."

"I'm sure we'll find a way to burn it off."

"Ha, I'm sure we will."

I loved how much I could laugh with Zack about anything. He wasn't insecure in any way, and the way he treated me made me feel really confident about myself. However, I couldn't get Sarah's words out of my mind about the twenty-something-year-olds. They're young, gorgeous and obsessed with image, with special thanks to TikTok, Instagram and *Love Island. Do I still need to compete with them?* Look at Max The Wanker. He was in a happy, secure relationship with my amazing friend, Sarah, who would have done anything for him, not to mention she's absolutely stunning, but his head was still turned by a twenty-something. *What guarantee do any of us have of a happy ever after?*

I wrapped the biscotti back up and decided to skip on more indulging this evening.

"So, what have you been up to today?" I asked.

"I called back at home today to make sure the place is still standing, which it is. My housemate hasn't burnt the place down yet. It's been a boring one, really. Miserable weather over here too, if you can believe that. How was the Colosseum?"

"Oh, it was amazing. There was some serious eye porn. I took so many photos. I'll have to show you when I see you, but they just don't do the place any justice at all. You won't believe how big it is. We'll have to come sometime, so you can see for yourself."

"Well, actually..."

"What?"

"I've got a confession. I've been before. Years ago, we went as a family and did the whole touristy thing."

"Why didn't you tell me? I've been bragging about how much of a good time I'm having here, and you've already experienced it. I bet I've sounded like a right idiot."

"Well, you can't help that." He laughed as I swore at him. "But it's fine. Rome is just... there are no words for it. Everyone needs to visit Rome at some point in their lives. And I love hearing how much you've enjoyed your break. We'll definitely go together one day. Did you see the Vatican too?"

"Yes, we went after we had our little picnic. That was a strange experience. I probably can't describe it properly, which doesn't matter as you've already been. But it felt quite eerie."

"I thought that too."

I took the phone out to the balcony and sat down at the table. The air seemed cooler tonight. There was a refreshing breeze. I put my feet up on the other chair and relaxed, talking to Zack about next week when we would both have the week off together. At least one of those days would be spent in bed.

I heard a familiar laugh and looked down over the balcony.

"I think I can hear Sarah," I whispered to Zack, as I leaned forward to watch the people below. "Yes, they're back, he's walked her home. Shh."

"Why are you shushing me? They can't hear me."

I spied on Sarah and Alessandro as they gazed into each other's eyes at the bottom of the hotel steps. I could only see the tops of their heads, but I knew they were smiling. He then raised his hand and stroked her cheek before leaning in for a kiss. *Wow.* I felt like I was in it. I could almost feel their body heat rising and ruining the breeze keeping me cool. He slowly pulled back and stroked her face one last time before stepping back to walk away. He made it only ten steps before he looked back to give her one final wave.

"I'll have to go, she's on her way up."

"Are you going to giggle and gossip about kissing boys, over biscotti?"

"Yes, in our pyjamas, right before we have a pillow fight."

"Well, just make sure to save me some biscotti, don't eat it all. Okay, baby, I'll speak to you tomorrow. Love you."

"Mwah, I love you too."

I stayed on the balcony waiting for Sarah to get to the room. I watched as the knob turned on the door and in she came, rosy-cheeked (finally!), eyes glistening and a smile from ear to ear. She hadn't noticed me staring at her from the balcony.

"Ahem," I called out, finally getting her attention. "Did you have a good evening?"

She didn't answer. She just nodded her head. No words were needed. Her sheepish smile said it all.

Sarah was back.

CHAPTER FIVE

Why does it always take forever for suitcases to appear on the conveyor belt at the airport when you arrive back in your own country? When you have been travelling for hours and hours and just want to get home to the comfort of your own bed, you're hit with all these barriers. A delay in leaving the plane, huge queues at security, and now, finally, the long wait for our luggage. We must have been standing there for twenty minutes waiting for our cases, and they still hadn't appeared. Our prebooked taxi would be leaving without us, or waiting with the meter running and costing us an absolute fortune. I'd been on a fair few holidays abroad and never, not once, had my suitcase been the first to appear upon returning home.

"I wish they'd hurry up, or we'll need to book another taxi, and who knows how long that will take," I said to Sarah, who was being oddly calm about the situation. I thought maybe she was still distracted by thoughts of her Italian friend. "Who did you say you'd booked with? Do you think you should call them to say we're still waiting for our bags?"

"Don't worry about it, it'll be fine." She tried to reassure me, but I hated this part of holidays. Not just because it was over, but because the process of getting home always seemed to take an age. It's always a shame when you have to check out of such a perfect holiday abroad, but as soon as you do, you always just want to get straight back home to your own bed.

There was suddenly a loud clatter as the conveyor belt began to move.

"Finally!" I said. "Now just to wait for our suitcases to come out last." *Not forgetting the biscotti stash.* I needed some sugar.

I was incredibly surprised when mine and Sarah's cases were among the first to appear.

"There! You can stop your moaning now. Your suitcase hasn't ended up in the wrong country. It's all here, stowaway biscotti too." Sarah shoved me, playfully. "Come on, let's move to the front or we'll miss them."

We were able to grab our bags without fail and wheeled them through the doors and out to the airport car park. Outside, it was cold, dreary and miserable. Much like my mood. It had clearly been raining, as there were puddles everywhere.

I was looking for an impatient taxi driver ready to charge us a fine for making him wait so long, when suddenly... I couldn't believe it.

"Zack?!"

I dropped my suitcase in a puddle and ran towards him, throwing my arms around his neck as he picked me up for a huge, much welcome and much-needed hug. He smelled delicious. I could just eat him.

"What are you doing here?" He was still holding me up as I put my hands on his face to make sure it was really him.

"I'm your taxi."

"I wanted to surprise you," Sarah said. "As a thank you for everything you've done for me. Letting me live with you, putting up with me trying to sort my life out, and taking me on holiday to Rome. I owe you so much."

"Aw, hun." Zack placed me back on the ground so I could hug my friend, trying not to get over-emotional, which was difficult as I was tired, hungry and a little bit chilly. I hugged my friend tightly, pleased that everything was finally working out for her, and that she was feeling better about life and herself.

"My dad is picking me up, so you guys can get off home." I spotted Sarah's dad in his car, waiting for her. He was on his phone but waved when we saw him. "Right." She picked up her bag. "I'll leave you guys to it. Jenny, I'll speak to you soon. Don't break him tonight, will you?"

She headed in the direction of her dad's car. Zack picked up my case and put his arm around me, leading me to his car. He kissed me on the head and held me tightly.

"Was I a good surprise then?"

"Yes, you sneaky sod. I can't believe you're here. I feel all gross though. I wish I could have had a shower or something before I saw you. Get all freshened up."

"Well, I think you look amazing. But if you really want a shower, I insist on getting in there with you to help, if you'll let me?"

"How can I refuse that?" We arrived at his car and he placed my case in the boot. "But you'll have to be thorough in your cleaning, if you feel up to the task."

"Of course, I always make sure I'm thorough." He closed the boot and turned to me, gripping my face in his hands, kissing me passionately. "Get in the car." He slapped my bottom and I giddily jumped in the front seat.

Absence makes the loins burn harder. We'd barely left my bedroom since getting back yesterday.

Food had been consumed in bed. My mother would be

cringing if I told her. However, I was all grown up now, and could make up my own rules. If I wanted to eat food in bed, I could eat food in bed. If I wanted to spend the day naked with my legs wrapped around my boyfriend whilst eating fried noodles, then I would do that.

"What time is it?" I knew it had to be mid-morning by now.

Zack reached for his phone.

"It's nearly three o'clock."

"What? How is it that time already?"

I felt like I should be up, being productive. I still had to unpack and do all my washing. Not to mention going to the shops for food to stock up my cupboards. I had also promised Sarah a trip to IKEA over the weekend, so she could continue to buy things for her new home. There were so many things to do, but my legs would not unwrap themselves from my sexy boyfriend, who was trapped between them. He didn't seem to mind, nor was he in any rush to get up either.

Suddenly, when all was peaceful and relaxed, I could hear my phone ringing. "Typical," I moaned.

"Where is it?"

"Ah, I think it's still in my bag, over there." I lifted my arm and pointed without looking. "Too far away to get up. It's fine, they'll leave a message."

"Okay, but I need to get up anyway, so I'll pass it to you. Do you want a drink?" He gently lifted my leg from his body.

"A coffee would be good, but I'll come down for it."

I watched as my naked boyfriend got out of bed and put on his clothes. I seemed to have gotten over my fear of the exposed penis in daylight. No longer did I mind seeing it walking around my bedroom in all its morning glory.

"I'll see you downstairs then." He smiled as he pulled up his pants and made his way out the door.

As the door opened, in came Bing.

"Hey, little man," I said, holding my hand out to him. He ran over and rubbed his face in my palm, purring. "Aw, I missed you too. Sorry for kicking you out of the bedroom last night. It's just, you know, three's a crowd."

I heard my phone bleep with the sound of a voicemail. I grudgingly threw back the duvet cover and got out, slipping on my dressing gown, which I found in a crumpled heap on the floor. Searching through my bag, I found my phone and listened to the message.

"Jennifer, it's your mother. Why aren't you answering? I assume you're back in the country by now. Call me back."

There's nothing like hearing the maternal and loving voice of one's mother. I thought about ignoring it, but she'd only call back again. And again. And again, before sending my brother around to look for me. *I may as well get it over with.*

"Oh, she *is* alive." My mother's warm greeting never fails to amuse me.

"*Buongiorno,*" I say, in my most Yorkshire accent. Perhaps some Italian culture would impress her.

"You got my message then? I'm impressed. It usually takes three calls, a voicemail and a Hogwarts owl for you to get back to me."

"Well Bing ate the last owl you sent, and the RSPB tried to sue me, so, what's up?"

"Your brother is having a barbeque at his house next Saturday. Just a small family do. I hope you're coming."

"He sent me a message about some kind of gathering last week. I said I'd be there."

"And Zack? Will he be coming?"

"I don't know, Lady Mother. Is he invited? I can ask him."

"Of course he's invited. Your brother hasn't met him yet, and it is about time he did. Make sure he comes too."

"Okay, but you'll be nice, right?"

"I don't know what you mean," she said, in her most innocent voice.

"So, you weren't dropping hints that summer would be a wonderful time for a wedding when you last saw him?" Zack found it hilarious, luckily, but I was less than amused when he had filled me in later.

"Oh." She paused. "He told you about that? That was just a big misunderstanding. A miscommunication. I was just saying, this summer is meant to be the best in over a decade. It *would* be nice for *a* wedding. I didn't mean you two, specifically. Any couple who might be planning some nuptuals, that's all."

"Just promise me you'll be tame. No more talk of weddings or babies, and I'll see if he's free to come along."

"I promise. It starts at one o'clock. Next Saturday. Their house. You'll be there?"

"I'll be there. Now I have to go, I've got things to do."

"One o'clock."

"I'll be there. Oh, wait, actually, *next* Saturday?" I jested. "I'd planned to get a huge tattoo on the back of my–"

"Jennifer..." She could go on *Britain's Got Talent* to demonstrate her skills in vocal tone change.

"I'll be there."

It was almost midnight and I was still wide awake. Zack was asleep next to me and Bing was curled up between my feet. I couldn't stop thinking. Zack had said yes to coming with me to my brother's gathering the following week. He was looking forward to meeting my brother, but I was dreading the whole thing. Andrew and I have always gotten along. As sibling relationships go, we had a good one. We never really fought as kids and I always covered for him when he was majorly hung-over after a night out so our parents wouldn't suspect. Of course, he returned the favour when I started going out too. In fact, by then, he took me under his wing and showed me the best places to go. He was quite the lad back in the day, but Elizabeth put a halt to that when they got together. He no longer goes out drinking with his mates, he's not allowed to eat processed meats, and he had to sell his favourite leather jacket because 'leather is cruel'. She gifted him a faux-leather jacket to make up for it. My mother slapped me on the leg when I pointed out that it was made from plastic, and so was more harmful to the planet than the genuine article.

I'd be lying if I said I didn't like Elizabeth. I liked her a lot. We had known each other for a long time. We even went to the same school, in the same year group. We weren't in the same circle of friends, but we'd always got on really well. She did go through some odd phases though. My brother always tried to justify them on her behalf, because he loved her, but I know my brother and he doesn't wholly convince me that he is on board with her ideas. I know he still grieves for that leather jacket. If they ever did get a divorce in the future, I'm certain he would pin the beginning of the end to that moment he handed it over to the guy who bought it on Facebook Marketplace.

It would be great to see my nephews, Sam and Ethan, again. They're close in age, but such different characters. To Sam, I am the cool aunt. We play games and his laugh is infectious. His little brother Ethan isn't sure about me yet though. He must get that from my mother.

I couldn't pinpoint why, exactly, but I had a feeling that my brother's barbeque would be very interesting.

CHAPTER SIX

Just the thought of going to IKEA makes me tired, but it is one of those places you have to go when you move to a new house. It's a necessary evil. I do believe they intentionally made the layout this way to test how committed we are to getting a hotdog. No one wants a BILLY bookcase this bad, it's got to be all about the hotdogs. If you make it out of the store without needing anger management, then a hotdog is your prize.

"Will you slow down?" I called to Sarah, as she whizzed her way around all the corners. "I'm going to lose you."

"Just follow the arrows and stop when you see the beds!" she shouted over her shoulder. She was on a mission. Forty-five minutes later she had found the bed she'd been staring at online for the last few days, and successfully ordered it for delivery the following week, along with a gorgeous wardrobe with matching bedside cabinets and a unit for her home office. Not forgetting a BILLY bookcase.

After spending the last couple of weeks sleeping on a memory-foam mattress on her bedroom floor, she had finally found the perfect bed for it, and it was clear she was pleased as we made our way through the checkout.

"Are you sure Zack won't mind helping to build it all?" she asked me as she took her receipt from the sales assistant. "I don't mind asking my dad to help out. There's a lot to do."

"He offered to help you out anyway he can, and so will I." I linked her arm as we exited the store. "He can help build it all and I can supervise and make the coffees. Perfect team." We both laughed.

"Have you heard from Alessandro?" I asked a little while later, over lunch at a bistro table outside a local café.

"Not much really, although he did check that I'd made it home safely," she said with a smile. "It was just a holiday fling, I think. It'd never work. Long distance is tough when it's another town, never mind another country. But it was such a good idea meeting up with him. Even though it couldn't have gone anywhere, I feel like I'm open to the idea of romance again."

"Woo, progress!" I lifted my glass of water to toast this victory. "Here's to getting back out there."

We toasted my friend's launch back into the single life.

"So, do you think you're ready for actual dating, or do you want to leave it for now?"

"I think I'm ready now," she took a sip of her Diet Coke, "it's just, where do you meet people these days? I know you met Zack at work, but I work in a very female environment. There are no guys. Well, none who are attracted to what I have on offer anyway. How am I going to... What's the matter?"

"I know what you should do." I dropped my fork beside my plate.

"What?" she asked, digging into her food. "Stop looking at me like that, you look possessed."

"I know what you absolutely *have* to do!"

The timing was perfect. She was finally healed emotionally, ready to move on. She had just bought her own house, so was feeling like the strong, independent woman I knew she was. Plus, it would be nice for the shoe to be on the other foot.

"Are you going to tell me, or what?" She looked scared.

I smiled. This was going to be fun.

"You, my dear most beautiful friend in the whole entire world, have to sign up to Find Me A Date."

"Absolutely out of the question." She shoved a forkful of chicken in her mouth.

"Why? You have to! You made *me* do it."

"That was different," she gulped down her food, "you needed a date to my wedding. No one we know is getting married, so I don't *need* a date."

"Yes, you do. You need some meaningless dates to get you back in the swing of things. Some harmless interaction just for practice, for when you meet someone you actually like."

"Why can't I just wait until I meet someone I like?"

"Because you'll be too afraid to make a move, like I was. You're doing this." I reached for her phone, before she could stop me. "You made me do it, against my will, not to mention those lovely guys you set me up with. This is payback."

I entered her passcode and downloaded the app before she could stop me. The 'Find Me A Date' logo hadn't changed, and I shivered at the memories of crude messsages. It was a rite of passage in the dating world and Sarah needed to experience it.

I handed her back her phone. She stared at me, defeated. "You're not going to let it go, are you?"

"Not until you've had at least one terrible date that I can laugh at. Come on, you owe me this at least. Or do I have to find some guys myself for you? I could always give Dreary Gerard a call? I'm sure he'd be available." After my terrible date with him last year, I would be surprised if he was off the singles market yet. I'd honestly rather have watched paint dry than spend another moment in his company.

"Fine," she huffed, and took her phone, typing in the answers to the basic questions and uploading a profile photo. She chose one from Rome, where she was standing with her back to the Trevi Fountain, her sunglasses on top of her head, one hand held up to shield her eyes from the sun. "There," she said, handing her phone back to me after a few minutes. "Are you happy?"

I studied her profile, making sure I approved of the answers, when...

Ping.

"Woah, already? Check *you* out," I said as the app suddenly pinged with a notification of someone liking her profile.

Ping: another like.

Ping: request to meet.

Ping: another like.

Ping: message request.

"These guys must be glued to the app waiting for fresh meat!"

"Let me see." She wanted her phone back, but I got the first look. I couldn't believe what I was seeing.

"Ha, typical. When I uploaded my profile, I got all the weirdos sending me crude messages. You're getting all the hot ones. Look at this one," I turned the phone for her to see, "Matthew, aged thirty-two from Leeds, veterinary surgeon. Unbelievable."

"Oh, he looks nice." She took the phone from me. "And look at this one too! Anthony, twenty-nine from Huddersfield, an audio engineer. Looks like he works at the local radio station. This might not be such a bad idea after all."

"Is everything okay with your food?" the waitress asked.

"Yes." Sarah smiled as I remembered I hadn't started mine, and began munching on a chicken wing. "It's great, thank you."

"Well, it looks like you'll be inundated with dates in no

time. Do you want to reinstate the code word in case of an emergency situation?" I couldn't remember how many times I'd had to send Sarah the infamous 'tea' message for an early escape.

"If I feel I absolutely have to, then I'll send you an SOS. Ooh..." She was distracted already. "Look at this one. He's already sent me a message to meet up."

She passed me her phone. Arthur was a thirty-four-year-old investment banker from Harrogate. He also looked the absolute spit of Boris Johnson.

"He looks like a long-lost love-child of Boris Johnson, right down to the hairstyle."

"Studied at Oxford though. Impressive, and very eligible, wouldn't you agree?"

"Looks like his pockets are probably lined with personally embroidered handkerchiefs from Harrods instead of dead rodents from under a bush." I wondered how Rob was getting on. My mum still doesn't believe me when I tell her the story from *that* date. "Go for it."

"I think I will." She typed out her reply to him and pressed 'Send'.

What's the worst that could happen?

CHAPTER SEVEN

Zack had offered to drive, but giving directions to my brother's house was far too complicated. Even Google Maps got confused by the postcode. *Who buys a house in the middle of nowhere, miles away from the nearest tarmacked road?* Andrew and Elizabeth bought their house just after they got married, thanks to a hefty donation from Elizabeth's parents and grandparents. The wedding, which was also funded by the in-laws, was held on an island off the coast of mainland Greece. Everything was magical and perfect. Although my favourite bit of the day was when the doves they released pooped on Elizabeth's mum's fascinator. Still, I don't recall having any cause to complain. The waiter Christos was barely old enough to serve alcohol, but was trained in quickly replacing an empty glass of ouzo with a new one.

As my car rolled over their newly gravelled private driveway, which was as long as my own street, we finally arrived at the house. I parked as far away as possible, delaying entering their perfect home, seeing their perfect children and having every family member commenting on how perfect everything was. Yes, Andrew's house was immaculate, but they all seemed to forget that I had grown up with him. I knew all of his quirks and disgusting habits which would certainly be grounds for divorce if he still did them now. I remembered his bedroom back home being so grotty that there was a family of mice living under the heap of clothes under his desk.

Thinking about my family, I had a sudden, unexplained pang of panic. "It's not too late, you know," I said to Zack, as he unbuckled his seatbelt. "We can leave now and say we couldn't make it. Too much traffic on the M62. There's always roadworks, or a crash to hold things up. No one would question it."

"I think it's a little too late for that, my dear." He patted my knee.

"Why?"

"Your mother has spotted us and is over there waving for us to hurry."

"Just don't make eye contact! Come on, let's go." I jangled the keys.

"Come on," he laughed, "it won't be that bad. It's only family. If someone starts asking you probing questions just shove some food in your mouth so you can't answer."

That was a very good point. This was a barbeque. Better yet, a barbeque hosted by my brother and his wife. Their 'no processed meats' rule meant there would be big, meaty beef burgers, pork sausages and strips of chicken coated in delicious marinades. Colourful salads and creamy pastas. My stomach grumbled at the thought of it all. I was so glad I'd skipped breakfast for this, as there would be a mountain of food on offer.

We got out of the car and Zack stared at the house. To be honest, it was more like a mansion. Surely no one needed that many bedrooms.

"This is quite a place," he said, taking it all in. "Makes my flat look like a shed or an outbuilding."

"I have to admit, it is really nice. Just don't ask Liz about it. She'll take you on a tour to show it all off, and that'll take about three hours. You'll miss all the food."

"You could save me a burger." He put his arm around my shoulders.

"If you want to risk leaving food alone with me, then it'll be your own fault."

He laughed and kissed the side of my head. The gravel crunched under our feet as we approached my mother in the doorway. She changed her expression from a scowl to a smile as she greeted Zack with a hug and a kiss on each cheek. She reserved this kind of affection for Zack every time she saw him.

"So nice to see you again, Zack." She turned to me, looking less friendly. "You're late."

She stepped back so we could make our way into the house. The entrance hall was the same size as my living room. There was a bespoke oak wardrobe for coats, a matching cabinet for shoes, a two-seater sofa, and even a piano in the corner. I often liked to sit in entrance halls and listen to music. Who needed a lounge?

"Nice to see you too, Mother. Were you really waiting for us at the door?"

My tummy rumbled. I could smell food cooking.

"I heard you coming down the drive. The food is almost ready, so you're just in time."

"Oh good, I'm starving. Seriously, Zack, my brother gets the best burgers. You'll love them." My mouth was already watering.

"Actually, there's something I forgot to mention," my mother said, shutting the door behind us and dropping the latch to prevent any potential exit.

"What? Don't tell me they didn't get any burgers?" I complained, already wishing I was out the door.

"Not quite." She wouldn't look me in the eye. "There are burgers, but not what one, or rather you, would usually have."

"Mum, what is going on?"

"They're, ah... Your brother and Elizabeth now eat a more plant-based diet."

"What the chuff is a plant-based diet? Are they cooking dandelions?" *Although, come to think of it, a garden weed would be far too common. They would be ordering bouquets of only the best flowers from the florist to eat instead.*

"They're... exploring a vegan lifestyle," she finally said.

An unplanned explosion of laughter left my mouth, only ending when I saw that this wasn't a joke. My mother was being serious.

"They're what?"

My brother. The one who lived on meat-feast pizzas throughout his three years at university. The one who ordered double-meat subs from Subway. The one who wanted a spit-roast pig at his twenty-first birthday party. *He* had given up all animal products? This had to be a wind-up.

"They've decided on a change to be healthier and more eco-friendly, so this whole barbeque has a vegan-only selection of food. It's actually rather delicious. Marvellous what these chefs come up with nowadays, you can't tell the difference. You should sample the bacon or should I say facon. Tremendous."

"So, they're going to save the planet by forcing everyone to eat lettuce and hummus? What if there's a greenfly on the lettuce and I accidentally eat it, will Liz ban me from the house?"

Zack scratched his chin in order to hide his smile.

"Don't be ridiculous, Jennifer, it won't kill you to try something new."

"Why didn't you tell me?" I could have prepared by eating something before I came.

"Because I know you, and you wouldn't have come at all. You would have found an excuse, something to do with that cat of yours."

She's right, of course. I wouldn't have come.

"It's not going to be full of hippies, is it?" I asked, envisaging walking out to the garden and coming face to face with the long-haired preacher who campaigns in the town centre come rain or shine.

"Don't be silly, it's just family. Now come on, everyone is waiting." She made her way through the door and out into the back garden.

"I tell you now," I whispered to Zack once she was out of earshot. "If I find a stray caterpillar in my lettuce leaves, it's having a public execution as a form of protest. What will they do if their kids get nits? Pull them out alive and set them free?"

"Wow, you do get cranky where food is concerned. It's quite cute, actually."

"My brother *isn't* vegan. I'll never believe it."

"Well, there's only one way to find out. Come on. If you get through this without making a scene involving a caterpillar and a guillotine, I'll treat you to a big bucket of Colonel Sanders' finest on the way home."

"With gravy?"

"Double gravy. We can have one each. How about that?" He placed his hands on my face and pulled me in for a kiss.

"All right, fine," I said, when we'd pulled apart from each other. "You're on. I promise I will try not to kill a caterpillar." If I saw an ant on the pavement though, it would need to run for cover.

We walked through the house, through the conservatory and out into the garden. With a sense of trepidation, I looked to the table where the food had been laid out.

Suddenly, a little person appeared in front of me.

"Aunty Jen! Aunty Jen!" he called out.

"Hello, Sam!" I picked my oldest nephew up and sat him on my hip. "Oh, you've grown."

Sam giggled as I tickled him whilst he was trapped in my arms. His brother, Ethan, stared up at me with his wide eyes, unsure what to make of me. He had some sass for a three-year-old.

"Who's that?" Sam asked, looking at Zack suspiciously.

"That's my friend, Zack. I've brought him to meet you all today. Do you want to say hello?"

Zack smiled. "Hi, Sam, I've heard a lot about you."

"Is he your boyfriend?" he asked, with a look of disgust on his face.

"He is, are you going to say hello to him?"

My crazy confident nephew suddenly went all shy. Zack tried to say hello to him again, but he was having none of it, wriggling out of my grasp and running to the safety of his parents. Andrew, the new patron saint of animal welfare, turned and waved before making his way over to us.

"Jenny!" He greeted me with a hug. "So glad you came, sis. Haven't seen you for ages. You never come over to see us here. And this must be Zack?"

"It's nice to meet you. Thank you for the invite." Zack shook his outstretched hand.

"Not a problem, pal. It's good to meet you, finally." He took a swig of his beer, which I noticed wasn't his usual brand.

"Erm, what's this?" I pointed at the bottle, his hand slyly covering the label.

"What?"

"This, right here, you might have missed it. It says 'non-alcoholic'. I thought you were allowed to drink on weekends if you were a good boy and did all your homework. Did you buy the wrong one by mistake?"

"Well, no, Elizabeth doesn't want alcohol in the house whilst she's breastfeeding." He looked around to see where his wife was. "If she isn't allowed to have it then it's not really fair."

"Ah, right, okay. I hear you. And this whole vegan thing is, what, because the baby can't chew on a steak yet, so it's not fair to rub it in her face?"

"Actually, a plant-based diet is *incredibly* healthy." He spoke loudly this time, turning to check where his wife was again. "No saturated fats, high fibre and, well, it's proven to improve health. What are you staring at?"

"Nothing, nothing," I said, although I had been staring at his mouth, waiting for the signature lip quiver to give him away. "So, who's here then?" I looked around, seeing a crowd of people I didn't really recognise swarming round Elizabeth as she cuddled baby Cora.

"Not many, actually. A lot of Elizabeth's friends made it. Had a few people cancel last minute. Uncle Roy said something about a job in his garden."

"Hmm, weird." I said, betting anything that it was the food on offer that had turned off many of his family and friends. "Well, you'd best tell me what food there is because I have no clue what you've put out."

"Me neither," he said, a lot quieter. "It's all a load of crap. I'll tell you where the sausage rolls and chicken drumsticks are hidden later."

"Jenny?" my mother called from across the garden. I saw she was holding Cora and making her way across to us, Liz eyeing her carefully as she made off with her baby. "Jenny, come see little Cora. Isn't she beautiful?" She finally reached us.

I peeked at Cora's chunky little cheeks as she was presented to me. "Aw, yeah, you did make another cute one, bro. Kudos."

"She is beautiful," Zack agreed.

"What are you doing?" I asked my mum, who was trying to pass the baby to me.

"Unfold your arms then. Come on, she won't bite."

"Yeah, Jen," my brother piped up. "Come on, you know you want to."

I shot him a glance as my cheeks burned.

"Here." Before I could protest, my mum placed the baby in my arms, which I reluctantly unfolded to cradle little Cora. She was sound asleep, luckily, and little squeaky sounds escaped from her tiny nostrils.

"See," my mother said. "Nothing wrong with that."

I smiled in agreement as I looked at the baby's face. Tiny specks of dark hair were visible on her head. I released one of my hands to stroke her, amazed at how soft her skin was.

"Looks good on you, Jen," Andrew teased.

"Yes, perfect practice for when you and Zack have..." I shot my mother a glance this time, hoping to silence her. "I mean, *if* you and Zack, not that you need to, you might not, or you might, but..."

"Come on, Mum." Andrew took baby Cora from me. "Help me see if Cora needs a nappy change. It must be time now."

"I didn't mean..." Mum tried to argue her case as my brother put her arm around her, pulling her away.

"Let's just head this way." Their voices faded as they made their way back into the house.

I looked to Zack who was trying, and failing, to hold in a laugh. "Are you okay?"

"Shall we investigate this food situation?" I said through gritted teeth.

"Ha, come on." He put his arm around me. "It'll take a lot more than your mother's comments to have me running for the hills."

~

"That wasn't too bad, was it?" Zack asked on the drive home. He insisted on driving.

"It wasn't too bad, my mother walking on eggshells the rest of the afternoon was quite funny. You handled that well."

"Your mum's harmless." He chuckled. "Anyway, you survived your first experience of vegan cuisine. What did you think?"

"It was all right," I said. "Off the record, though, I am bloody starving." I smiled at him, and he took his eyes off the road for a second to glance back at me. I loved his smile. "Anyway, how did you get on? I saw you chatting to my brother for ages. I wanted to be nosy and see what was so interesting between the two of you, but I was otherwise engaged."

"Yeah, I noticed you'd been roped into a game of hide-and-seek with Sam. He's adorable."

Sam had been hiding behind a tree for ages, his arms wrapped around it, which meant it was glaringly obvious where he was, but he really believed I couldn't see him. If his arms weren't giving his position away, his infectious giggle was.

"It was fun, but I admit, I was trying to stay away from my mother. She kept trying to make me hold the baby again. I mean, yes, Cora is incredibly cute, but I prefer them when they can talk." Zack laughed. "Do you know what I mean though? Babies are silent, you never know what they're thinking or when they're going to spit up on you."

"You might feel different when it's your own in the future."

"Mum? Is that you? Your Zack mask is very convincing." I prodded his face.

"Ha! You know what I mean."

"Yeah... I guess."

His words knocked me back a bit. He didn't say 'our baby'.

Did he mean that I would have babies in a future without him? Or was he planning that kind of future with me? We've never talked about having kids. We've never even talked about getting married. He *has* practically moved in with me since I got back from Rome. We haven't spent a night apart. I know the tenancy is up on his flatshare soon. Did he want to renew it, or make it official and move in with me? Apparently, grown men are as silent as babies when it comes to what they're thinking. I might have to tickle it out of him, like I had to tickle Sam to tell me where he had hidden my phone after I'd let him play Candy Crush on it earlier.

"Perhaps." I didn't know how else to respond.

"I was chatting to your brother about holidays. He said they'd not been abroad since having Sam."

"No, I think the thought of controlling that many children on a flight gave Elizabeth an anxiety attack. Shame really. They had some fantastic holidays before they got married. They actually took three months off work and travelled around Asia for their honeymoon." I remember my mother being in a panic as they went during monsoon season and we lost contact with them for a few days. It turned out they'd made friends with a local taxi driver who took them in. Only my brother could have ended up in that situation.

"Maybe we should go away together. What do you think?"

"Really?" I had visions of us buying a tent, camping in a boggy field and trying to heat up tomato soup over a poorly lit campfire. "Yeah, that could be nice."

"There'll be some late summer deals. Portugal is nice, have you ever been?"

"No." I suddenly perked up and momentarily forgot all about my hunger pangs. "Have you?"

"A few times. Or we could look at the Canary Islands. Where would you like to go?"

"Anywhere I can relax by a pool or dip my toes in the warm sea and feel my skin sizzling under the sun." I smiled. Rome was amazing, but I felt like I needed another holiday to get a rest as soon as we got home. A relaxing, romantic summer getaway, just me and Zack, would be perfect.

It may not be one of the more serious relationship questions like babies or marriage, but going on holiday together is a big commitment. We could wake early and, in true Brit style, nab our sun loungers before everyone else and then head for breakfast. Sunbathe, swim in the sea, more sunbathing, eat as much food as possible. Then, before it was time for our evening meal, we would head back to the hotel to shower and have sex.

"Great. We can get looking soon, get some ideas." He took his left hand off the steering wheel and put it on my leg, leaving it there whilst we cruised down the motorway.

I heard my phone ping through the Bluetooth connection to the car. I'd not checked it since Sam brought it back from wherever it had been hidden. There were two missed calls from Sarah and three WhatsApp messages.

Tea.

TEA.

FFS WILL YOU CALL ME, TEA TEA!!!!!!!

Oops. I had already failed in my duty.

"I forgot that Sarah was meeting someone today. She mustn't be enjoying herself much." I couldn't contain my giggles.

"Aren't you going to call her then?"

"Okay, okay, I suppose I ought to rescue her."

It was probably time to put her out of her misery.

"What took you so long?" Sarah asked me breathily when I finally called her.

"It wasn't *that* long," I laughed, "only an hour. Little Sam had my phone, sorry."

"I could have been kidnapped and murdered in that time. Although that might have been preferable. Oh Jenny, it was bloody awful. Just awful. I forgot how terrible the dating scene could be."

"Given how much I complained about it, that does surprise me."

"I couldn't get away quick enough. I am mortified."

"So, go on then, tell me what happened?"

Sarah had opted to wear her floral maxi dress, with her hair down, bouncing off of her sun-kissed shoulders as she strutted in her stilettos. There was a group of men in their early twenties by the bar, making the most of the two-for-one drinks offer. They all looked up as she walked in, smiling at her as she removed her sunglasses. She wondered if one of them might be Nigel, her first dating app suitor, but none of them advanced towards her. She decided to wait at the bar and order herself a small glass of wine, when a tap on her shoulder stopped her.

"Oh, I don't need a table just yet," she told the very young waiter. "I'm waiting for someone, so I'll hang by the bar until he gets here."

"Sarah?" the young man said to her. "It's me, Nigel." His braces sparkled under the chandelier light and his black bow tie sat slightly wonkily against his white, creased shirt.

Sarah thought this must be a wind-up. That Jenny had arranged this as a joke. It had to be. Nigel's profile photo had depicted a normal enough guy in a suit, seated at a computer desk, holding a tumbler with what looked like a shot of whisky in it. Very suave and mature. The man standing in front of her did not look like he was old enough to legally drink alcohol.

"Our table is over there, by the window," he panted excitedly. Sarah looked to the group of guys by the bar, hoping they would

notice a damsel in distress and save her, but they had now been joined by a group of twenty-something girls and were no longer interested in her. They were sipping their cocktails and laughing together without a care in the world, and with no concern for Sarah at all.

Sarah followed her date, feeling like a childminder. He ran ahead and gallantly pulled out her chair for her, which she quietly thanked him for, secretly wishing it wasn't a table by the big window, but rather one at the back where no one could see her.

"So," Sarah began. "Nigel, I have to be honest, you're not what I was expecting."

He blushed and smiled broadly, clearly taking it as a compliment.

"How old are you?" she asked. She knew she sounded blunt, but she wasn't happy.

"I'm twenty-two. I know my profile says thirty-two. I need to change it."

"Yes, you do. And, just guessing now, but I suppose you're not a creative director at a web design company?"

"Well..." A waitress appeared before he could answer, with a plate of sandwiches, nibbles and cakes. Sarah was confused because they hadn't ordered anything to eat yet. "I hope you don't mind," Nigel said, seeing her obvious confusion. "I thought it would be nice to share an afternoon tea. I know women like that. I saw it on TikTok."

"Ah, I'm not familiar with TikTok."

"Oh you should get it," he insisted. "It's ace."

Sarah moved her attention to the food, which she thought looked very nice. She wondered if concentrating on the food would make this date more bearable.

"There are two glasses of prosecco included per person," the waitress said. "But as it is a special occasion," she winked at Sarah, "I'll just bring you a bottle."

The waitress sauntered away.

"Special occasion?" Sarah asked. "Why did she say it was a special occasion?"

"Well, when I booked here, I said it was our first romantic meeting," he made a sound which could only be described as a nervous giggle or a snort, "and I wanted it to be extra special."

She felt so embarrassed. It was time to bring out the big guns. She had rescued Jenny many times, having to take the fake emergency phone call, even if it was not convenient at the time. It was a duty. Now, it was time for Jenny to return the favour.

Sarah's phone was in her bag. She reached in and discreetly typed out the infamous text message and sent it. It would not be long until she was saved and could make a swift exit to the train station just down the road. She didn't want to just run out. Nigel was very young, and she didn't want to upset him.

The waitress had managed to compose herself long enough to bring over the bottle of prosecco and two glasses, however the tears of laughter were still in her eyes.

"Here you are," she said, gleefully. "Is there anything else we can get you to make your time with us more memorable?"

"No," Sarah said quickly. "This is memorable enough, thank you."

Sarah poured herself a glass of prosecco and wondered what was taking Jenny so long to call her back. She quickly typed out another message.

"So, I don't know if you recognised my name, or saw this on my profile, but I'm a bit of a celebrity around here," Nigel said, waiting for Sarah to ask him to elaborate. She stayed quiet, but he continued anyway. "I run my own blog. It's very popular. My last one got two hundred hits!"

"Oh yeah?" She picked up her glass, her eyes glancing to her *bag, impatiently waiting for the sound of her phone ringing. "What do you write about?" She glanced down at her Apple watch too, willing it to light up with a message, but nothing happened. She sipped her prosecco. It tasted like fizzy, sour water.*

"It's a sex blog."

"Sorry, a what?" She wiped some prosecco from her chin as she stifled a laugh.

"A sex blog. I write about my personal experiences. It has a huge following." His hand gesture as he uttered the word 'huge' made Sarah want to laugh even more. "So, just a heads-up, I am up for anything." He smiled, licking his lips. "I mean anything."

Sarah cringed. She wanted to be sick. She wanted to leave. She wanted her best friend to hurry the hell up and call her back! She sent another message, not caring if Nigel saw.

I was laughing so much I could hardly breathe.

"And then! He proceeded to tell me about the best position for reaching an orgasm if in a confined space such as a toilet cubicle. After that I was too scared to use the loo in case he followed me! He also mansplained oral sex, and I think I can confidently say from his explanation that he's never experienced it, giving or receiving."

"Stop!" I was finally able to speak. "Please stop, I can't take any more. This is too funny."

"I'm deleting that app."

"No, you're not," I insisted. "It was the first date. You've popped your blind-date cherry. It is time to find your second date."

"Do I have to?"

"Absolutely. This is fun, I can see why you sent me on so many. We just need a better vetting system. I'll help you find your next one. But most importantly, what is Nigel's blog link? I *have* to see it."

"I have no idea, I was too scared to ask. Anyway, if you read it, it might put you off sex forever. I stopped listening when he tried telling me how to find the male G-spot. That is the time your emergency call *finally* came through, so I still don't know the answer, thank God. Tell me something to get my mind off the thought. What did you do today?"

"I ate vegan food at a vegan barbeque."

"Shut up. You? I don't believe you."

"Well, believe it. I'm even thinking of converting. I have seen the light, and the light is leaves mushed up and shaped into sausages."

"Now I *know* you're lying. You'd never give up bacon sandwiches."

She knows me far too well. I told her about my brother's secret stash of meaty treats in his garage. He managed to briefly take me in there, telling his wife he was showing me his new Tesla, when he really wanted to show me the storage cupboard, which was actually an integrated fridge.

"That's hilarious."

"Why doesn't he just do what he likes? That's what I don't get. He always seems to go along with what she wants. It's like he doesn't have a voice in his own family environment." *It was the same with my own parents. There never was any middle ground.*

"That could be marriage," Sarah said with a sigh. "Not like you or I know anything about that. There'll be sacrifices and compromises. As long as everyone's broadly happy. Maybe having a happy wife is what makes Andrew happy."

"She has a new trend to try every year. You watch, she will want them all to live in a mud hut in the middle of the woods, without electricity or running water next."

Sarah laughed. "I think that's a bit extreme. Although I still remember their wedding breakfast, with the food served on banana leaves."

"Ha! My mum still hasn't gotten over that. It didn't help that I told her to watch out for exotic African spiders hiding in amongst them. Anyway, I need to share my most exciting piece of news..." I hesitated, leaving Sarah in suspense while Zack parked up. I motioned to him that I'd be in shortly. "...Zack has asked me to go on holiday with him."

"Ooh! How exciting! When are you going? Where will you go?"

"I'm not sure. Somewhere hot and sunny, walking distance to the beach, food on demand, private pool, balcony optional."

"You're not asking for much then." She laughed. "You'll get some good deals this time of year too, I bet."

"Hopefully. I think we'll get looking properly over the next few weeks. We just need to get this meal out of the way with his parents, first."

"You're meeting the parents too? This is a night of big news. When's this happening?"

"I don't know, he's just got inside so might be giving them a call now. I'm so nervous. I get the impression they're really well off. I hope they don't suggest somewhere posh to eat. Those places always serve tiny portions of pretentious food. Do you remember your Aunty Susan's wedding in York?"

"Oh yes," she said, laughing. "When you made me sneak out with you to the KFC down the road before the evening guests arrived?"

"I was starving! That piece of pork was so small it may as well have been served on a cocktail stick."

"Well, find out where his parents want to take you first, and check out the menu. Then eat before you go if you have to."

"That's a good idea. Anyway, we need to meet up soon and find your next date."

"Believe it or not, I'm not in any rush for that, but we do need to meet up. How about after you've met his parents? We could do lunch and you can tell me all about them."

"That sounds like a plan," I said with a smile.

I put down the phone, allowed myself a couple of moments to dream about a hot holiday with Zack in the not-too-distant future, and then headed inside to put the kettle on.

CHAPTER EIGHT

I am a reasonably sensible, somewhat mature, thirty-one-year-old woman. I work in customer services, actually dealing with members of the public on a face-to-face basis, giving them joyous news that they can't have what they want, and why they can't have it. Needless to say, there is an element of crowd control and diffusing difficult situations involved. I have faced many obstacles in my life, not to mention living on my own all these years with a cat I was sure wanted to kill me during the first few years of being roomies. So, after all that, why was I suddenly terrified of meeting my boyfriend's parents? They're humans. Two humans who produced the love of my life. Two humans who supposedly already liked me before they'd even met me. Why was I so nervous? *Because I knew how much it mattered to Zack that it went well tonight.*

I was even more nervous because one of the nicest restaurants ever had been chosen for this momentous occasion. I had never been to Alice Garden before, not since I read the menu online and saw they charged over nine pounds for a small glass of wine. The food looked amazing on their online menu though. There were no tiny portions to be seen. I still had some making up to do with my digestive system after attempting vegan food, and had promised my stomach a big, juicy steak. Although, I wouldn't want to be burping in front of Zack's parents. What would they think of me? With names like Alistair and Miranda, they were sure to be posh.

We managed to find a parking space close to the restaurant. When I got out of the car, I checked over my dress to make sure I wasn't covered in Bing's white hair. Using my phone's front camera, I checked over my make-up too, not wanting my eyeliner to appear smudged. I also needed to keep my phone close by. Sarah was on another blind date, and I had promised to call her straight away if she needed to escape, this time.

"Are you all right?" Zack asked, putting his arm around me to lead my resistant body to the restaurant.

"Yes, yes, I'm fine," I lied, almost choking as my mouth and throat felt really dry.

"That's their car." Zack pointed to a silver Porsche Carrera. "Dad loves that car. Mum wanted him to sell it as it sits in a garage for six months out of the year. But he can't part with it."

"Why can't *you* have it?" I said, trying to stop myself from drooling all over the bonnet.

"Ha, I asked my dad that a few years ago... He still laughs about it now. Come on, they'll be waiting."

He held my hand and squeezed it reassuringly as we walked up the stone stairs and through the door.

"Hello and welcome to Alice Garden," the hostess said. "Do you have a reservation?"

"Yes, we're meeting my parents." Zack pointed to the table near the bar, where two very smiley people waved at us, and the waitress led us to them.

"I'll be back shortly to take your drinks order." She smiled.

Zack hugged his parents. It was very loving and affectionate. Not something I was used to myself.

"Mum, Dad, this is Jenny." He was so comfortable in their presence. Again, not something I was used to personally.

"Hi, it's so nice to meet you." I almost curtsied. Then I remembered – this was not the time to be a tit.

"Hello!" His mother stepped forward. "I'm Miranda." She pulled me in for a hug. It felt wonderful, very mumsy. "We're so glad to finally meet you! We've heard so many good things." Her smile was so genuine, and I felt instantly at ease.

"I'm Alistair. Would a hug seem too awkward or..." He held out his arms and I laughed.

"No, no, it sounds great!" I said, leaning in to hug him.

"Let's sit, and let's get some drinks ordered," Alistair said as we pulled apart. "I've never been here before, but it's very busy, which is always a good sign."

"Can I get you anything to drink?" The waitress had returned.

We each gave our drinks choices. Miranda and I ordered the same glass of wine so decided to share a bottle instead, and the guys ordered Italian beer.

"Jenny," Miranda began. "Zack tells me you own your own house. Is that true?" She seemed impressed.

"Yes, it is."

"I've been wanting Zack to buy a house for years," Alistair said. "But he never listens. Now house prices and interest rates have shot up, he'll have to wait until they come back down. The market will be up and down for a while I expect."

"Well, it's so difficult to get on the property ladder these days," I said. "My friend Sarah was lucky to get her house recently. But if I'm honest, I was only able to buy my house because I inherited half of it when my dad died. I got a mortgage for the other half, buying it from my brother."

"Oh, I'm so sorry about your father." Miranda looked mortified. "Alistair, stop talking about houses and finances."

"It's fine, it was a long time ago," I said, worried I was bringing the mood down on the evening. "I grew up in that house... well, until my parents split up anyway. So, when it became empty, it was up to me and my brother what we wanted to do with it. He didn't really want it, I did, so I bought it." It was great to get some distance from my mum, too. Living with her was becoming a challenge. Even with the rise of bills year after year, the cost of my sanity was more important than the cost of living.

"Sad circumstances, but a great position to be in," Alistair bravely piped up. "You made a very sensible decision. We like to surround ourselves with intelligent people." He smiled at me.

"Thank you." I was beaming. I never got the same praise from my own mother. All *she* could say was, *"You'd best change the hallway carpet, that's where your Dad's dog died in a pool of its own urine."*

Fifty minutes and four delicious plates of food later, we were all relaxed and enjoying each other's company. I couldn't believe I had been so nervous to meet them. Miranda and Alistair were great. They were so easy to talk to and seeing Zack with them had made me love him even more. He was so respectful and polite, especially with his mum. *If a man can respect his own mother, he will always respect you.* That's what my grandma used to say. And she was right.

The conversation had moved on to holiday destinations. Zack mentioned that we had discussed booking a break for September. We still hadn't found anywhere yet, there was so much choice. I liked the idea of a Greek island, but there were so many to choose from.

I felt my phone buzz in my bag. When I checked it, it was a message from Sarah, with that one famous word. It was time to rescue her once again.

"I'm so sorry," I said, "I just need to make a call. Will you excuse me?"

As soon as I stood up, Zack and Alistair stood up in unison. It felt like I was an important lady at the dinner table in *Downton Abbey*. How very proper.

I smiled at the hostess, as I nipped out the glass door and to the bottom of the steps.

"Hello?" Sarah's voice answered before I could speak.

"Hey, it's me, there's a huge comet flying towards earth about to land on your car. You might want to park somewhere else."

"Oh no, that's terrible!" Sarah's A-level in drama was paying off. "I'm coming right now. Don't move, I'll be right there. I'm so sorry," she was talking to her date now, "I have to leave. Let's rearrange, okay? Goodbye." I heard a lot of muffled noise before she came back on the phone. "I'm back, I'm outside now. Oh my *God*, that was creepy."

"Worse than your sex blogger?" I kept my voice low so the patrons still entering the restaurant couldn't hear me.

"Much worse."

"He wasn't a vegan, was he?"

"Shut up," she said, laughing. "It started really well. I had high hopes for this one. He was a fitness instructor. Very hot body. Very nice to look at, but..."

"But what?" I glanced inside and saw Zack's parents smiling as they spoke to him.

"He was fitness obsessed. When we were looking through the menu and he asked me what I fancied to eat, he'd tell me how many miles I'd need to run to burn it off. But it wasn't even disguised as a fun fact. He was *actually telling me* I would need to burn it off, because it would be a shame to let myself go. After all, I am in my thirties, so my metabolism won't be what it used to be. Those are the actual words he used. Can you believe it?"

"What an absolute dick!" I said it a little too loudly, aware that the restaurant doors were open so I could be overheard. That kind of language isn't very *Downton Abbey*.

"Where are you? Can I come over?" she pleaded. "I feel like popping to the shop for a chocolate fudge cake and ice cream. I could send him a selfie of me eating it. Fancy sharing one?"

"I can't. I'm out with Zack and his parents. I just nipped outside to rescue you."

"Oh, I forgot! How's it going?"

"Really well. I'll call you tomorrow and tell you, but I love them."

"Aww, that's so good! Just a heads-up if you order any pudding, you'll need to do a good four- to five-mile run if you do. In fact, best just avoid it altogether at our age."

"Ha, ha, I won't be following such a rule. Speak to you tomorrow."

"Bye!"

I ran up the stairs and arrived back at the table.

"Is everything okay?" Miranda asked.

"Oh yes, my friend needed a quick word, but she's fine. Thank you."

"Zack," Miranda said, putting her hand on her son's. "Why don't you see what Jenny thinks to our idea?"

I looked at Zack, who seemed hesitant.

"Mum has suggested that we all go away together in September. They have a villa in Crete and were already planning to go for a month or two. It has four bedrooms, two living rooms, three bathrooms, and a tennis court. It's a shared pool, but only with one other villa. Very close to the beach. We'd only need to pay for the flights. What do you think?"

"Don't feel pressured," Alistair said. "If you kids want your own holiday, that's fine by us."

"It's very private," Miranda said, clearly hoping we would

join them. "And we wouldn't need to be under each other's feet. You can do your own thing when you like. All I ask is we try to eat together in the evenings. We had a new kitchen put in last year, but there is a barbeque too."

"If you like lobster, you'll like it even more on a barbeque," Alistair said with a smile.

This sounded amazing. How could I refuse?

"That sounds like a great idea. I'd love to."

Zack beamed.

"I'm so glad!" Miranda clapped her hands. Her smile stretched from ear to ear. "This calls for a toast. Shall we have one more drink before we call it a night?"

CHAPTER NINE

There was always a mid-week lull at work, right before the lunchtime rush where everyone in the vicinity who had a thirty-minute lunch-break wanted to rush to the council offices to report their problems of overgrown grass verges, loose flagstones on pavements, and complain that their neighbours were playing their music too loud and wanted me to personally visit to sort it out.

"Thanks," I said, as Cheryl handed me a hot cup of tea.

"You're welcome." She took her seat next to me and looked to the empty waiting area. "Depressing this, isn't it? Knew I should have booked the day off. Could have got a manicure or something. I might book a week or two off next month."

"Not September," I pleaded. "Me and Zack are going away for two weeks then, but I don't know the exact dates so haven't booked the time off yet."

"Oh, that sounds exciting." She swivelled her chair to face me. "Where are you going?"

"To Crete." I blushed as I smiled. "His parents have a villa and have invited us to join them. He showed me photos of the place last night and it's like a mansion. Absolutely stunning. I can't wait."

"Sounds very serious, holidaying with the parents. You kids are adorable." She took a sip of her drink. "Ooh, this is hot. Uh-oh, we have a live one." An elderly gentleman was walking down the corridor to the waiting area. The stick in his left hand looked older than he was, and I was worried it would snap from under him. "Bless him, it's Mr Corby. He gets slower and slower every time. I wonder what non-council issue he wants to complain about this time."

"I'll see him if you want, you did it last time." We usually took it in turns to see the regulars like Mr Corby. At his previous visit, what would usually have taken three to four minutes reporting a street light being out became extended to how things were back in his day when council workers gave no mind to health and safety regulations and would just climb a ladder to change a lamp. He had a point. Our own caretaker needed a certificate before he was allowed to repaint a wall inside the building, so that he couldn't sue the council if he was poisoned by the fumes.

"No, no, I don't mind. He's sweet really, reminds me of my grandad. Hey, Mr Corby? Come on over, love." She managed to catch him before he got to the chairs, which was good as he always struggled to get back up once he'd sat down.

I jumped as I heard my phone ringing. Luckily, the manager was nowhere to be seen, so I couldn't be scolded for forgetting to put it on silent.

"I'll be right back," I whispered to Cheryl, as Mr Corby took his seat and I sneaked away.

I heard Mr Corby begin his rant about the neighbourhood children being too loud as I pushed open the door to the corridor and answered Sarah's call.

"Hey, is everything okay?" Sarah wouldn't normally call me at this time.

"He's asleep," Sarah squealed down the line.

"Who's asleep?"

"My date."

"Your... your date?" I glanced again at the time on my phone. "It's not even lunchtime, what are you doing on a date?"

"It was the only time he could spare," she huffed. "I took an early lunch-break for this and he's bloody asleep. What do I do?"

"Okay, start again, you've totally thrown me here. Who are you with and why on a Tuesday morning?"

"The other night I was back on that dating app and everyone was just, well, gross. This guy called Piotr kept sending really crude messages and wanted me to send him nudes. Anyway, I thought, *I'm not doing this*. Dating apps are new-age rubbish, people used to actually meet each other in person once upon a time. You know, in the old days. So, I went to Lidl."

"Ah, Lidl, the breeding ground for eligible bachelors wanting freshly baked sourdough bread." I tried some recently. It was amazing.

"Well, where else did people used to meet each other and fall in love? Didn't people used to bump into each other in the street and then get married?"

"So you went to the Lidl middle aisle, hoping to meet someone who would take you down the matrimonial aisle?"

"It was really late, but I couldn't sleep. I was short on a few things so thought I'd go down to Lidl. Grabbed a basket and walked around. Anyway, I noticed this really good-looking guy."

"Not Nigel the tween then?"

She chose to ignore me. "He had an NHS lanyard around his neck and was wearing a shirt and tie, so I figured he must be someone important. A consultant, perhaps. He was at the pineapples, picking them up one at a time. I noticed he didn't have a wedding ring on, so I decided I needed a pineapple too."

"Of course, we can never get enough pineapples. Did you buy one? We can make piña coladas."

"Anyway... I picked one up and my hand just *accidentally* brushed against his. You know how it goes. '*Oh, I'm so sorry*', I said. We had a laugh and a mid-aisle chatter. Compared pineapples. He's a surgeon, had just finished a shift. Ten hours in surgery repairing someone's spine who had fallen off a motorbike."

"Ouch." I cringed.

"I know, I could understand being tired after that, poor guy."

"I meant 'ouch' for the dude on the motorbike, but never mind, carry on. Your hot surgeon without a wedding ring was buying a pineapple."

"Well, we were flirting for about ten minutes until he finally asked me out, but the only time he could do was this morning. He was working all night and he's on again later, so we agreed on a brunchy-type thing, but he's fallen asleep."

"Oh, what a shame." I once fell asleep during a training session a few years ago. I couldn't help it, so easily done. "Are you on your way back to work then?"

"No, I'm still here."

"Wait, you're still there? And he's asleep?"

"Yep, he's got the fork in one hand, his head in the other, and he's asleep. It's been about fifteen minutes. I've already taken a photo. I'll send it to you on WhatsApp later."

"Why are you still there then?"

"Jenny, the food here is amazing. It's a new tapas place in Leeds. You should take Zack sometime."

"Sounds like a great atmosphere if Dr Pineapple has fallen asleep. Or maybe you were too boring," I said, laughing.

"Sod off, I was my delightful self. Anyway, you'll be pleased to know that after this disaster, I'm going to give the dating app another try. I just need a better vetting system to avoid the fitness obsessed and the, well, Nigels."

"I can help if you like?" I offered. "What time do you finish work today?"

"I should be done by four o'clock. What are you thinking?"

"Fancy meeting me when I finish at five? There's a Wetherspoons not far from here, we could have a cheap and cheerful tea and then go through the app."

"Oh, yes." She thought about it. "Yes, actually that's perfect. I can show you a photo of Dr Pineapple. I think you'll be impressed. Oh... shhh."

There was a muffled sound.

"Sorry," she returned, "I thought he was waking up, but false alarm."

I jumped as the door opened behind me.

"Sorry, hun," Cheryl said. "Could you come back? Mr Corby is still on one about the reliability of the old gas street lamps, and there's a queue forming behind him."

"I'm on my way!" Cheryl disappeared back to the office. "I'll have to go, it's getting busy. Do you still need help putting furniture together this weekend?"

"If you guys don't mind."

"Not at all, Zack's looking forward to it. He even went back to his flat to get his toolkit."

"Thank you, I owe you both a meal out. I might bring you to this place, actually."

"I'm not sure about that, I hear people fall asleep in your company. See you this afternoon."

CHAPTER TEN

I was grateful that the office had quietened down by the end of the day as it meant I wouldn't be delayed in getting away on time. Zack had phoned me to say he'd been called into a last-minute meeting so would be late back to my house too, so I fully expected Bing to be a pain in the arse later. Sarah had texted me to say she was already at Wetherspoons and had secured us a booth. This way we could sit together and go through the dating app. Perhaps we could make alterations to her profile and make it clear the age group she was looking for so there could be no more Nigels weeding their way into her dating life. Although I do wish I'd been able to read his blog.

"Hey!" I found Sarah and slid into the booth next to her. "I'm so hungry, only had a ham sandwich for lunch today. Can we order straight away?"

"Course we can," Sarah said. "Go ahead, I'm not that hungry. I ate Dr Pineapple's food as well as my own before I left."

"How long before he woke up? He must have been mortified."

"Well, unless the staff woke him up, there's a chance he's still there."

"You left him asleep?" I was both shocked and highly amused.

"Of course I did!" She laughed.

"I can't believe you. I'll be back in a minute, I'll go order. Are you sure you don't want anything? I doubt that fitness instructor you dated is in here, so there's no one to shame you if you want a bowl of chips."

"Go on then," she said. "Get me some chips, and maybe some chicken goujons. I'll go grab some condiments when you get back."

I walked over to the bar and just as I gave my order, I stepped to the side and almost bumped into a young man. He barely looked old enough to be in there.

"Sorry," I said, as my shoulder grazed his.

"Don't worry." His voice was nasal. "Accidents happen." There was something about him I couldn't quite put my finger on. Something familiar. "Is that Sarah I saw you come in with? Sitting over there in the booth?"

"Sarah? Yes, it is. Do you know her?" I looked over at her, but she wasn't looking our way.

"We had a romantic rendezvous. I must speak to her."

Before I could stop him, he was making his way over to an unsuspecting Sarah.

"Wait," I called out.

"That'll be fourteen pounds and eighty pence," said the barman, holding out the card reader.

Dammit. That was absolutely one hundred per cent Nigel on his way to speak to Sarah and I was going to miss it!

As soon as the payment transaction was completed, I rushed over to our booth so I could witness the alleged sex blogger in action.

"Jenny, you're back!" Sarah was relieved at my return. "I'm so sorry, Nigel. We were having a private catch-up, so..."

"No, don't apologise." He had slid into the booth, making himself comfortable in my space. "I was just telling Sarah how much I enjoyed our date but, unfortunately, I don't think another one would be sensible."

"Really?" I had to bite my lip. I looked at Sarah, who rolled her eyes at me. "Why's that, Nigel?"

"Well," he began, as I sat on the other side of Sarah. She kicked my leg as I joined her. "Although Sarah is obviously a very, very beautiful lady, stunning in fact, I don't think she is quite what I'm looking for in a partner."

"Oh, no, that's so sad! What a shame. She had been filling me in on your romantic meeting." I winced as Sarah nipped me under my arm. "Sarah, are you okay? Do you need comforting?" I put my arm around her tense shoulders.

"I do think it's for the best," Nigel continued. "I certainly need someone not as advanced in their years."

Sarah stiffened, and I willed myself to remain composed until Nigel had left us alone.

"I don't think any more needs to be said, do you, Nigel?" Sarah threw him a look that could kill. "Maybe we end things here, and never speak of them, or to each other, ever again."

"You're upset, I understand," he said. "It's never nice to hear when you're not compatible with someone. I will leave you ladies to your talk."

Sarah's shoulders relaxed as Nigel finally moved away from her.

"Oh, Nigel, before you go, can I ask you something?" I beckoned him back over.

"Of course." He faced me.

"Sarah told me you write a very, very successful sex blog. Famous, in fact. I'd love to give it a read."

"Oh my God," Sarah whispered under her breath.

"Yes!" He fumbled in his pocket, pulling out a business card, which he handed to me. "Please, leave a review. Especially if you try the Flying Eagle. I need feedback. Actually, ladies, I have a project in mind if I may discuss it with you both. You may be up for taking part. I'm looking for two older women who wouldn't mind…"

"Goodbye, Nigel!" Sarah's voice was loud enough to get the attention of the bouncer near the door.

"I can't believe you did that," Sarah said as Nigel finally walked away. "I cannot believe you took his card. We are not reading that blog."

"We absolutely are." I laughed. "What the hell is a Flying Eagle?"

That weekend, Zack was doing a grand job at reading the instructions and constructing Sarah's new furniture, and I was doing a grand job of making Sarah jealous about my upcoming two-week getaway to an all-expenses paid villa in Crete. Plus, in amongst all the commotion of our midweek post-work get-together, we had completely forgotten to discuss her dating profile.

"Two whole weeks?" she said as we were sitting on her new sofa drinking wine. We were flicking through profiles on Find Me A Date, but not having any luck. "Don't say more, I might actually turn green."

"Did I mention it has a tennis court?"

"Since when do you play tennis?" She laughed.

"Never." I sipped my wine. "But when in Rome. Speaking of Rome, have you heard any more from Alessandro? Does he keep in touch?"

"Occasionally," she said, as she swiped through the app. "We have the odd 'How are you?' chat and briefly tell each other what we've been up to, but no more than that really. He did hint about chatting on FaceTime though. Oh, what about this one?" She handed me the phone. "Twenty-eight years old, a postman–"

"Swipe left," I interrupted. "Postmen get up early on a morning. You don't need that on a Monday. Next."

"But he was so hot! Imagine him slipping a parcel into your letterbox." She pouted. "You're so picky."

"No, I'm experienced in this business. And if anyone messages you wanting to video-call, tell them no."

"Are you girls okay, or do you need a rest?" Zack popped his head into the room. "Wouldn't want you to tire yourselves out."

He walked into the room and leaned down, kissing me on my head. "Sarah, I don't suppose you have any scissors? I can't find mine in my toolbox."

"Oh yes," she got up, passing me the phone, "I'll get you some." She ran down the hall and up the stairs to the loft room, which was home to many unpacked boxes. I asked if it could still be classed as a bungalow if it had steps to an upstairs room. Apparently, it can.

"How are you getting on?" I asked Zack.

"Almost there, just the wardrobe is a bit awkward." He wiped some sweat from his upper lip.

"Do you need any help?" I felt guilty. Sarah and I had spent the whole evening gossiping whilst he got on with putting all her stuff together.

"No, it's fine. Enjoying myself, actually. Won't be long now."

"Got them!" Sarah called from 'upstairs'.

"Coming." Zack left and made his way to meet her.

I carried on swiping through the profiles. Most of them were the same delightful guys from when I'd had the app. Left. Left. Left. *Woah, what? Is that who I think it is? It can't be. It is.*

Dan.

I couldn't believe what I was seeing. Dan had a profile and was looking for a relationship. I guessed he was as serious about wanting to settle down as he'd said he was when I last saw him.

"You look like you've seen a ghost." Sarah joined me again on the couch.

"I think I have." I passed her the phone and whispered, "It's Dan."

"Dan who? Your old 'buddy' with the waterbed?"

"Yes."

"Oh right, how funny." She had a glance at his profile. "He's looking good. I'd forgotten what he looked like." She reached for the bottle of wine and passed it to me so I could top up our glasses while she continued studying him. "Well, if he's single, he's allowed to mingle."

"I know, I just wasn't expecting to see him on there." I poured out the remaining wine and placed the empty bottle down. "Good luck to him."

It had been a while since I'd even thought about Dan, but thinking about him now, looking to date other people, made me feel uneasy. It was always weird seeing ex-boyfriends with other people, but Dan and I were never boyfriend and girlfriend. We didn't end things with an argument or a fight. We just... ended.

"What did it say on his profile?" I asked, curious. "I didn't read it properly. I was scared it'd swipe by accident and accidentally send *you* on a date with him."

Sarah clicked back onto his profile and read it aloud.

"My name is Dan and I am thirty-two years old from Halifax, West Yorkshire. I work as a senior mortgage advisor. I've had fun over the years, but now looking to settle down with the right girl who is also looking for love."

My heart almost melted.

"*Ideally,*" she continued reading, "*someone similar in age and with a love of hiking in the Dales. I would love to find someone I could consider a best friend as well as my girlfriend.*"

"Bless him," I said, "I didn't know he had that in him." Also, I'd had no idea he was a senior mortgage advisor. I thought he was something in IT. If I'd known, I would have gone to him when my mortgage was up for renewal.

"You had a real impact on him it seems. '*Also looking for love*'. Sounds like you broke his heart and he needs someone to heal it."

"Don't be daft," I knocked her with my foot, "I didn't break his heart. We just wanted different things."

"Yes, he wanted you, and you wanted the office eye candy who's currently building my furniture." She laughed. "Can't blame you for that, but let him get on with it. If he knows what he wants, and you're his friend, let him find someone and be as happy as you are."

We clinked glasses and I remembered the all-important question I had to ask her. "Speaking of doing huge favours for your best friends, could you do one little, tiny, minuscule thing for me?"

"Go on." She looked at me suspiciously.

"Please could you watch Bing for me while I'm away? Call in and check on him every other day and make sure he has some food? Fresh water? Maybe make sure he hasn't planned world domination from my kitchen?"

"Why doesn't he just come and stay with me while you're away? He doesn't like being on his own anymore, does he? I can work from home some days, so he'll have some company."

Bing hated being home alone now. Only I could get a cat that suffers from anxiety and depression. Staying with Sarah would be the better option. "I don't know if that's such a good idea. I'm scared he'll claw at your brand-new couch or something. I don't want to put him in a cattery, though."

"It's only two weeks. I'll leave him in the kitchen if I have to go out, where he can't do much damage. You should bring him around here, it'll be fine."

"Are you sure?"

"Absolutely. It'll be a good test. To see whether or not I'm ready for my own pet."

"I wouldn't measure that kind of commitment against having Bing in your house." Bing is not your normal household pet.

"Sarah?" Zack called from the bedroom. "Which wall did you want the wardrobe up against?"

"Hang on, I'll be right there."

Sarah ran out of the room. I picked her phone back up, looking at Dan's profile. It was a good photo. His hair was neatly cut and he was wearing a black shirt. He looked very grown up. Very different from the Dan I remembered, although he was usually naked when I saw him. Good for him.

After Zack had finished building Sarah's furniture, we finally arrived back at my house. Bing had been asleep on the windowsill and ran to the door to greet us as we came through, rubbing himself on our legs until Zack gave in and picked him up for a snuggle.

"Do you want some Dreamies?" he said, cradling my once human-hating cat. "Come on, let's get some Dreamies." He placed him back on the floor and they walked into the kitchen together, side by side.

Bing's white tail flickered from side to side at the mention of his favourite treat. Zack was so at home here. I'd been back from

Rome for a few weeks and we still hadn't spent a night apart. It had become normal for him to just come straight here after work and stay over, and I loved it. His tenancy was almost up on the flat. There was no point in him renewing it and paying rent and bills for a place he spent no time at. We'd met each other's families, he loved my cat and helped out my best friend without hesitation. And yet... I was nervous about broaching the subject with him. *I was about to ask my boyfriend to move in with me.*

I walked into the kitchen, where Zack was feeding Dreamies treats to Bing, one at a time.

"Do you fancy a coffee?" I asked, wondering how to bring something like this up.

"Yes, please." He gave Bing his last treat and brushed the crumbs off his hands. He came up behind me and put his arms around my waist.

"So, I was thinking, you've been here a lot lately haven't you?"

His body stiffened, and he held me at arm's length. Crap. This was going wrong already.

"Are you getting sick of me?" He laughed, nervously. "I can go back to mine if you need a night to yourself."

"No! Oh my God, no." I turned to face him. "That came out so wrong. What I'm trying to say, is... what I mean is, we're always together, here." His eyes widened as I struggled to find my words. He had no idea where I was going with this. Hell, I don't even think I knew where I was going with this. Word vomit was threatening to make a tit out of me, when what I really wanted to say was, "Do you want to move in? Properly? Officially?"

His face relaxed, he released a long breath and finally smiled.

"I thought you were subtly trying to tell me you needed a break from me. Which is fine! I'd understand."

"I'm sorry." I laughed, covering my face with my hands to hide my reddening cheeks. "I'm so bad at the serious stuff, but I want you to move in. I know you've been here every night recently anyway, but let's make it official." It was my turn to put my arms around his waist. "Do you want to live here? Officially?"

"Officially, yes, I do." He leaned forward and kissed me. "Wow, we have our first holiday abroad coming up and we're moving in together as well. This is a very grown-up year for us. We're only in our thirties. What will your mother say, I wonder?"

"She would probably remind me that at my age she was married with two kids, had a dog and was just about ready for her inevitable divorce." I laughed. "And then she would tell me something about my brother. Like how one of his toddlers is bound for Oxford, while my cat is bound for the asylum."

As though he knew we were talking about him, Bing hopped up onto the kitchen counter beside us and was eyeing up the bag of Dreamies, which Zack had left on the side.

"You've had enough," I said to him as he moved his gaze to Zack, eyes wide and whiskers flared in his direction. "I said enough." Bing ignored me and continued looking at Zack. "I suppose I don't need to consult with him whether or not you can move in, he loves having you here. I think he'd vote for me to move out if it meant you could stay."

Zack chuckled and moved his hand to Bing's head. Bing leaned into it as Zack scratched between his ears.

"I do love your cat," he said.

"Aw, we're getting soppy in our old age, too."

Clearly repulsed by our act of soppiness, Bing hopped down and walked away.

We kissed again. I couldn't believe how happy I was feeling. A year ago, I never would have believed anyone who said that not only would I be kissing Zack in my kitchen, but that he would actually want to move in with me. And with only a few weeks until our holiday, things could not get any better.

"What's that noise?" Zack and I had been embracing for a few minutes, but an all too familiar sound had made its way down the hallway and into the kitchen, disturbing the peace.

"Bloody hell," I said. "Bing. I'll go sort it out." Reluctantly pulling myself away, I followed the noise as Zack continued to make our drinks.

It was the all too familiar heaving sound of a cat throwing up, but where? That was the fun game. I crept carefully down the hallway, hoping there was nothing disguised in the beige carpet.

"Oh my God," is all I could say.

"What? What's happened?"

Zack came running to the bottom of the stairs and found me with my hands covering my face. All I could do was point to our coats, which were in a heap on the bottom step.

"Are you *sure* you want to move in here?" I managed to say, before I involuntarily gagged at the sight of a combination of hairball, Dreamies and various stomach contents spread over our coats.

"Huh, too many treats do you think?" Zack asked, guiltily. "I'll sort these out." Zack carefully scooped up our soiled coats and took them up to the bathroom. He passed a proud-looking Bing on the top step. "Not cool, bro. Not cool."

Bing looked down at me.

"Don't look at *me*," I said to him. "*You* pissed him off, not me."

CHAPTER ELEVEN

With just seven days to go, Samantha had allowed me to work half a day today, or rather she was getting sick of my holiday talk and didn't put up much of a fight when I asked to leave early, so I decided to nip home to get changed and then headed out to buy some last-minute holiday bits. There might be some bikinis in the sale. A few more couldn't hurt.

It was a humid day today. I hated trying on clothes when I'd been this warm. I wondered if I could manage to fit in a quick shower before I set off. I would be in a better mood for shopping if I felt fresh.

Zack was finishing work early too, but had decided to go straight to his flat to do some more holiday packing and make a start on sorting out his things for the big move, so wouldn't be with me until later on tonight. We'd decided that the official move-in date would be when we returned from Crete, so there wouldn't be any need to rush to get all his belongings across. We could just focus on the holiday.

I'd be on my own for tea today for the first time in ages. I wanted to try to be healthy so I didn't put on any unwanted pounds before the big holiday, but with the choice of easy, delicious fast food on offer at the shopping centre... So much temptation.

I ran through my front door and threw my keys on the stairs, not wanting to waste a moment so I could get back out as soon as possible.

"Bing!" I waved my hand for him to come inside, but he just ignored me and ran down the driveway before I could grab him. "Oh, fine. Stay out there then." I was still a little annoyed at him for throwing up on our coats. Of all the places in the house, particularly all the places with laminate floor where things can be easily wiped up, why our coats?

I heard Bing's cries through my open bedroom window as I dried myself after a quick shower.

"I'm coming," I called to him, as he wailed louder than usual. There was no shade, so I bet his little paws were burning on the tarmac. He usually liked to sit under the table, protected from the sun and looking out over his territory like a king, but not today for some reason. "I'm coming, Bing."

Within minutes, I was pulling on my comfy white pumps, grabbing my bag, and running down the stairs to let the cat back in, but something about his cry grabbed my attention.

"Here you are, you silly sod," I said to Bing as he ran into the hallway. He let out a meow that sounded more like a moan. And another, louder one. He stopped in his tracks and shook his head from side to side. "What's the matter?" I dropped my bag on the floor. There seemed to be something in his mouth. "Come here." I knelt on the floor beside him, but he turned away from me and growled. Even by Bing's grumpy standards, this was out of character. "I can't help you if you don't let me look. Come here," I said again more firmly, getting worried. His mouth was wide open, drool was dripping on the floor. He seemed agitated. Had he been bitten by something? He liked chasing spiders, it would be just my luck that he found the only black widow spider in Yorkshire.

Out of his mouth dropped a wasp, desperately trying to cling to life. Its wings moved slowly as its legs tried to find some grip on the floor, which was covered in Bing's saliva. Without hesitation, I grabbed a discarded shoe and whacked it without mercy.

I looked back to Bing whose eyes were wide. There was a pool of drool by his feet now and he was panting heavily. His little cheeks started to swell. Was it possible to go a year *without* this cat causing some potentially expensive drama?

Pulling out my phone, I quickly called the vets who, let's face it, may as well have been on speed dial by now, and explained what had just happened. The receptionist put me on hold to speak to the vet, returning within a minute, telling me to bring him in straight away.

This was going to be pricey.

I left Bing in the hallway so I could retrieve the flatpack cat carrier from under the stairs. Hunched over, he didn't move. He was too focused on breathing to worry about what I was doing.

"It's okay, Bing, it's okay." I opened up the carrier, getting angry at the zips for not cooperating with my shaking fingers, until it was finally open. I effortlessly scooped Bing up and placed him gently inside, hearing him growl at being moved, but there was no attempt to put up a fight. That was an angry growl. I hoped it wasn't Dr Stevens on duty today. Please, don't be Dr Stevens.

Dr Stevens opened the door to his treatment room and scanned the waiting area full of people and their pets of all shapes and sizes. He did notice me sitting with Bing. However, he seemed to purposely avoid making eye contact with us. He approached the receptionist, who pointed in our direction. The colour drained from his face.

"Do you want to come this way?" he said with very little enthusiasm.

I followed him into the room and placed the growling carrier on the examination table in front of the reluctant vet.

"So, do you want to tell me what's happened?"

I relayed the story to him. "Do you think he's having an allergic reaction?" I asked, panicking. Bing's breathing could be heard from inside his carrier.

"I'll... I'll have to examine him." I could sense his apprehension. Vets were supposed to love and respect all animals, however, this was no normal animal. This was Bing. And Dr Stevens bore the scars to prove it. "Has he vomited at all? Diarrhoea?"

"No." At least I couldn't smell anything going on in his carrier. With fur as white as Bing's I'd surely notice something. "Nothing like that."

"Do you..." He exhaled loudly, preparing himself for what had to come next. "Do you want to get him out and I can have a look. It was in his mouth, you say?" He stroked his scarred hand, remembering the horrors of Bing's teeth.

"Yes, definitely in his mouth. The wasp just flopped out onto the floor."

Bing came out of the carrier very easily. He seemed disorientated, but clearly in pain, which was awful to witness. I think even the vet was feeling sorry for him. Without instruction, I held on to him so he couldn't move, knowing Dr Stevens was going to have to look in his mouth.

Carefully, oh-so carefully, Dr Stevens opened Bing's mouth, knowing that he had a duty of care to this savage animal. Bing allowed him to look inside with a small light, but only for a few seconds before pulling away.

"Well, I think he's only been stung the once, which is good, but it's on the back of his tongue," Dr Stevens said, removing his gloves. "It's swollen, which is why he's struggling to breathe, but there are no signs of an allergic reaction. I can give him something for the pain, to see if that helps to relax him a little, while the swelling goes down. But in a few hours, tomorrow morning at the latest, I expect he'll be back to normal."

"Oh, thank you." I smiled. "That's such a relief. When he was hunched over and struggling to breathe, I really panicked."

"Cats are notorious for getting stung by wasps and bees. Mostly wasps. Bees have the sense to fly away. Wasps fight back and then, well, this happens. And always this time of year too, when wasps are everywhere and cats see an opportunity to chase and pounce."

I watched as Dr Stevens prepared a small injection that would hopefully give Bing some comfort.

"Well, thank you so much for seeing us. I know he isn't your favourite patient."

"I can't deny that Bing and I haven't always seen eye to eye, but you never know, we might be best friends one day." He turned around with the needle ready. "Before that day comes though, do you want to hold him down again? Just in case."

As Zack was away for the evening, I called him on the way home from the vets to fill him in on the drama.

"Is he all right? Does he need to stay there overnight?" He had been so concerned for his buddy. "I can come back if you want?"

"Not necessary, he's on the back seat in his carrier growling to himself, so no different to normal." I sighed. "So, it looks like I can't go shopping now. I'll have to go on this posh holiday with my old raggy clothes and out-of-date bikinis. I hope they still fit."

"Whatever you have will be absolutely fine, I'm sure," he said. "You always look amazing, so please don't worry."

"Thank you," I turned into my road, "I'm almost home. I'll leave you to your evening."

"Call me if you need anything."

When I'd got Bing home, he stumbled out of his carrier and ran into the living room and on to the sheepskin rug by the fire, curling up into a ball. I brought his food and water to him, so he didn't need to go too far if he woke up hungry or thirsty, and then settled myself at the kitchen table to call Sarah. It rang several times before she picked up.

"Hello?"

"Hey, are you busy?" I asked. "I was wondering if you wanted to call over for a coffee and keep me and Bing company?"

"Oh, well actually," she hesitated, "I just wanted a quiet night tonight. Do you mind?"

"Of course not, it's last minute. Blame Bing, he went to battle with a wasp and ruined my shopping plans. Are you feeling okay?"

"I'm just tired. I had a full day of meetings, just one after another." I heard her hold back a yawn.

"That sounds rubbish. How's the dating app going?" I hadn't heard about any impending dates since we last went on it together.

"It's going okay. There was a guy who messaged me who seems nice... normal, even. We might be arranging something for tomorrow."

"Oh, exciting! Tell me about him. It's not the postman, is it?" I teased.

"Ha, no, not him. I'll tell you about him after I meet him. We've spoken quite a bit, sent a lot of messages back and forth. We were messaging until one o'clock this morning actually, which probably wasn't the best idea and it's probably why I'm so tired now." She stopped to yawn again. "Alessandro has been quite chatty too. We had a phone call the other night. It was nice to hear his voice again."

"You should go back to see him," I suggested. "Take a few romantic days away."

"Ha, maybe. He suggested that too. Have you started packing for *your* romantic holiday? One week to go! I bet you're so giddy now."

"Not packed yet, plenty of time for that, but I'm so excited. And now he's moving in I can't tell you how happy I am. There's so much to look forward to." I smiled to myself. "Oh, we need to arrange a date to bring Bing over before I go. When is best for you?"

"Ah yes, bring him anytime, I don't mind when. You've got a key so you can just let yourself in if I'm not here." She yawned again.

"Sorry if I'm keeping you up. I'll get off if you want to relax for the evening."

"Don't say sorry. I'm fine, honestly, just had a long day and think I'm getting a headache."

"Don't worry. I'll leave you to rest and we'll chat later."

"Call me in a few days and I'm sure I'll be feeling better. And we can finalise a day for you to bring Bing over."

"Sounds like a plan. Speak soon."

I put my phone down and went to check on Bing, who was now in a deep sleep on the rug. This time last year he had gone missing, and I'd spent so long worried about where he was and what he was doing. This year, he decided to sample a live wasp. I wondered what drama he would bring on us all next.

CHAPTER TWELVE

It was almost eight o'clock. I needed to give Sarah a call so we could plan bringing Bing over. It was going to be a major mission. A full, strategic plan of action was needed to make it as swift and smooth as possible and I needed to make sure the cat sitter was prepared. I'd been looking forward to speaking to Sarah for another reason. I wanted to find out more about the guy she had been messaging on the dating app. I hadn't even thought to ask his name. She hadn't sent me any emergency 'help' messages yet, so either they hadn't met up, or she had met him, and it all went well, but if so, why hadn't I heard anything about him?

She'd also hinted about chatting with Alessandro too, was something more going on there?

She picked up the phone after the first ring.

"Hello!" She sounded her usual happy self. In fact, she was possibly slightly happier than usual. "Five days to go, eek! I bet you're so giddy now and driving everyone mad."

"Oh, don't. My stomach doesn't know whether it is excited or nervous," I said. "I barely know his parents and now I'm going to spend fourteen days with them. I've only just felt comfortable enough to fart in front of Zack, now I need to hold it all in for two weeks."

"How much are you farting these days?" She laughed.

"You know what I mean! I can't embarrass myself in front of them. I don't even know if they know he's moving in with me. It'd be just like me to slip up and give it away somehow."

"Don't worry about it! You're both grown-ups, you're allowed to live together in sin. No one bats an eyelid anymore. Just relax, be yourself, don't fart too much in their company, avoid sex on the balcony and you'll be fine."

"I'll try," I said, ignoring her reference to our Zante disaster. "Anyway, we won't be stuck to them for the entire holiday. They said that as long as we're together for some evening meals, we can do what we like. I guess it's their holiday too, so they'll want to do their own thing without us."

"Exactly, so stop stressing. Just think about how you'll be sunning it up for two weeks with your office hunk. This time last year, you never could have imagined you'd be going abroad with him, never mind about to *live* with him. Just enjoy this break. No work to deal with, no politics, which is plaguing the news at the moment, just you and him for fourteen sunny days. And if you get a little bit worried, just give me a call. You know I'm here if you need to rant about anything."

"I'll need to learn the Greek word for 'tea'. Speaking of phone calls..." Here was my window of opportunity. "The last time we spoke you were telling me about your new dating-app interest. How's it going? Any progress?"

"Oh, there's not much to tell really."

"There must be something," I pushed. "Have you met up with him yet?"

"We went for a drink last night, it was nice."

"Well, I didn't get a 'tea' message, so it *must* have been." *This was great news.* "What does he look like?"

"He…" She hesitated. "He's tall. Dark hair. Early-to-mid-thirties, I'd say. Quite an alternative dress sense, like he was probably into the *Kerrang!* scene in the noughties."

"Nothing wrong with that." I smiled to myself, thinking about my love for Green Day and Good Charlotte. "Sounds like we'll really get on, which is great! I love when friends and boyfriends all get along. We'll be able to go on double dates and everything."

"Yes, well, it's too soon to plan ahead really. I don't want to jinx anything. We met once and it was great. We chatted for hours and we text every day. I'll fill you in after your holiday. We can meet up and I'll tell you all the juicy gossip, or spill all the tea, whatever it is the youths call it."

I sat back in my chair, still giddy that Sarah could finally have met someone perfect. Someone decent. Someone who she likes so much she doesn't even want to risk jinxing anything.

"Okay, okay, just promise me you will tell me *everything* when I get back?"

"I promise," she said, "I'll tell you all about him."

"Good." I was satisfied, knowing that my friend was happy. "So, when can I bring the great white savage feline around to you? We fly Thursday morning, so I can call around on Wednesday evening with him and all his stuff if that's all right?"

"Yes, I'll be free then. I'm meeting my friend again on Tuesday night, so Wednesday night is great, just promise me you won't try and interrogate me until after your holiday. Don't be sniffing around looking for clues."

"I don't know what you mean! Just ignore the webcam attached around Bing's neck, won't you?"

"Ha, ha. Very funny. Have you packed yet?"

We chatted for the next twenty minutes. Sarah dodged every attempt to mine for more information. I did respect her decision though. Mine and Zack's first few dates were one disaster after another. I hoped that over the two weeks that I was away, things progressed for her and this mystery man.

~

"So, tell me more about the villa." I lay my head on Zack's chest as we relaxed in bed the next morning. "What does it look like? Whereabouts is it? How many bedrooms did you say there are? Tell me all about it again." I was eager to visualise it, as Zack didn't have any more photos to show me.

"Ha! Okay, it's pretty big, I guess. It sits on a piece a land about a mile away from the sea, so we can have some beach days if you like. The outdoor pool is shared with a neighbouring villa, which is owned by some family friends. They might be there too, this time of year, with their daughter. My parents usually invite them over a lot to eat with us."

"I won't have to entertain the daughter, will I?" I can see it now – some bored, pain-in-the-arse teenager. Or worse, younger. So much for relaxing in a peaceful, private pool.

"Chloe is capable of entertaining herself by now. She's twenty-five."

"Oh?" Alarm bells began to ring, but I couldn't understand why. "How well do you know her?"

"I've known her all her life. We always spent our summers together out there. Our parents are very close. She's cool, very funny. I think you'll get on."

"Oh, good," I rolled my eyes, thinking back to Sarah's theory about the twenty-something girls taking all the good men. "Yes, I'm sure we will."

I rolled over, away from him, not wanting to show him the worry on my face. I'd just washed all my holiday clothes, but I couldn't be seen in a bikini with someone six years younger than me. I'd have to walk around all day with my arms up in the air, just to make sure my boobs were pointing the right way. He said they used to spend their summers together. Could they have slept together? All that playing in the pool while in bathing suits, is it only natural when you're young to hook up in that situation? *Should I ask him? Am I being paranoid? I wonder if it's too late to call Sarah.*

"Hey, why have you turned away?" Zack spooned me, a perfect fit, making me smile and relax once more.

Suddenly, Bing let out a howl at the bedroom door.

"He'll be hungry," I moaned. "I forgot to feed him when I got home last night. I should sort him out soon, or else he'll do his impersonation of Pavarotti. The neighbours will think we're harbouring a werewolf if he carries on."

"How's his *Nessun Dorma?*"

"Painful."

Zack laughed as he held me more tightly. "Do you have to right now? A few more minutes."

Bing wailed louder.

"Yes, I think I have to." I threw back the duvet and pulled away from Zack's arms. He rolled back over to his side of the bed whilst I put on my dressing gown.

Bing followed me downstairs, attached to my leg like a magnet, and he did not shut up until I had topped up his bowl with some cat biscuits. I made a mental note to warn Sarah that he can get very hangry.

I found my phone sitting on the kitchen counter, so I sent Sarah a message:

> Possibly sharing my holiday with a twenty-something... send me words of encouragement to stop me binning my bikinis! Xx

Almost immediately, she replied:

> Sod the twenty-something! You are fabulous! Gorgeous! Boobs never looked better! You make those Victoria's Secret models look like crap! Xxxxx

> A bit too far… but I appreciate the effort. You looking forward to your date tomorrow? Xx

She didn't reply instantly, so I popped the kettle on and set out two cups. I undid my dressing gown, looking down at my naked body. I was slumped forward, which wasn't a flattering look, my belly all rolled up and ancient boobs sat atop the flab. I stood up straight, pushing my chest out. My boobs still didn't look great though. I blew some cold air on them, making them look a little bit perkier. *Hmm, not bad. Still got it.* I just needed to make sure I walked around with my chest pushed out the whole holiday and… *Oh shit.*

I quickly closed my dressing gown, turning away from the elderly EVRi delivery guy who was staring at me, wide-eyed, through the kitchen window.

"Oh, bugger!" In my haste to fasten my dressing gown, I had pulled it around me quickly, but one of the ties swung around too fast and whipped one of the cups onto the floor. It smashed into pieces, scaring the life out of Bing, who slid on the lino in panic, unable to find a grip so he could run away quickly enough. My kitchen was suddenly a scene from a Looney Tunes cartoon.

"What's happened?" Zack rushed into the kitchen, looking around. His hands gripped my arms, as *my* hands covered my face in shame.

"Oh, nothing, I just showed off the goods to Fred. Full-frontal everything. Nothing major." My face burned, as I turned back to see Fred waving a parcel, unable to speak any words.

Zack, holding in his laughter like a gentleman, went to the back door and signed for it.

"I've heard of tipping delivery guys, but I think he got more than he deserved," he said afterwards. "This parcel isn't even for you, it's for next door. What the hell do you offer when it's for you?" He laughed.

"Sod off and make the drinks. I'll clean these broken bits of crockery up."

"Leave that, I'll clean it up." He reached down to the cupboard under the sink for the dustpan and brush. "You go back upstairs. I'll make us a drink."

"Okay, thank you." I leaned down to kiss him on the top of the head while he crouched down and swept up. Then I picked up my phone and read Sarah's delayed reply.

> Feeling quite nervous about the date, eek! I will tell you all about it when you get back from your holiday, I promise. Just need you to keep an open mind. xxx

An open mind? What could she mean?

CHAPTER THIRTEEN

One day to go. One final day to go. This time tomorrow, we would be on our merry way to beautiful, exotic Crete.

I'd allowed myself a bit of a pamper day today seeing as though I've been off work. I am now waxed everywhere I could possibly need to be. My legs have never been so smooth. The underarm wax was interesting and something I would prefer to never experience again. The bikini-line wax went a little further than usual, which was painful, but I don't want to risk an awkward moment if I'm going to be around a twenty-something who will probably look perfect. Although I have made a deal with myself that I won't think about that and make myself feel inadequate or insecure. I am feeling great and in absolute holiday mode. Nothing could bring me down today. Not the rain lashing down outside, not the empty fridge meaning there was nothing to eat, and not even the horrifying memory of flashing Fred everything I had to offer (pre-wax... even worse).

All of Bing's things were ready. I'd bought a new bag of his favourite food and grabbed a few of his toys and favourite blanket so Sarah's home could be a bit more comfortable for him. Although finding him is going to be an issue. Cleaning and packing up his litter box gave him a clue that he'd be going away somewhere, which was probably a mistake. I'd have to check under my pillow shortly. No doubt he'd be under there, moulting.

Zack wandered into the kitchen and opened the fridge.

"It's empty," I said.

"We don't even have any milk for a drink," he said with a sigh. "We'll need a coffee in the morning before we go. And a breakfast of some sort. We need to set off at five o'clock."

"Say what, now?" I stopped in my tracks.

"We need to set off at five o'clock." He looked at me as though I should have been aware of this traumatic news. "The flight is at eight, it takes roughly forty-five minutes to get to the airport. I doubt there'll be traffic at that time, but I need to check my car into their car park as soon as we get there. We'll want to be setting off at five, if not even earlier."

"I thought the flight was at eight in the evening?"

"We looked at a few flights, didn't we?" *Did we?* "And we decided to go with the earlier one so we'd have more time in Crete." I vaguely recalled a conversation about flights, but I didn't remember agreeing to such a demonic time. Zack pulled out his phone and started scrolling through his emails for the booking confirmation. "Here, see?"

He passed me his phone, so I could look at the flight details on his email. Sure enough, we had booked the eight o'clock flight in the morning. Dammit. Day one of my holiday and I'd be up before the birds. I started calculating. I'd planned on a morning shower, but if we'd be leaving here at five, I'd need to get up at four. Actually, no, half three. *Half three? Who gets up at half three? We may as well not be going to bed at all.*

I started counting the time on my fingers, but could feel myself flapping. Panicking. I'd planned it all out, but now I couldn't decide what to do. What would I do about taking Bing over to Sarah's? We'd planned to do it this evening, but if I had to go to bed early...

"Are you all right?" Zack stared at me.

"I'm just trying to work things out, don't you worry. Silly girly preparation stuff."

"Okay, well, you ponder over girly stuff. I'm going to pop to the shop for a pint of milk and grab us a pizza for tea. Unless you want to order a takeaway tonight?"

Hmm, a takeaway tonight meant a potentially irritable bowel situation on the plane tomorrow. All this last-minute panic was flipping my stomach already.

"Just grab a pizza from the shop, that'll do." *Probably the safest option.*

He kissed me then grabbed his keys and said he wouldn't be long.

I decided that I would shower before going to bed, so I could get up a bit later in the morning. It just meant I would need to take Bing over to Sarah's a little earlier than planned. I checked the time. She would be at work, but I could just take him over now. I had a spare key for emergencies, and I knew she wouldn't mind.

I tried to call her, but there was no answer. I wandered around the kitchen and tried again. Still no answer. I decided to send her a message and then leave, even if I hadn't heard back from her.

> Hey! Change of plan. I'll explain later but I'm going to have to bring Bing over now. I'll leave him in your kitchen with food and water, and I'll set up his litter box. Really hope he isn't any trouble for you! Ciaooo Xx

I quickly got dressed and made sure all of Bing's things were in my car. All that was left to do now was grab the escape artist. I made sure my arms and legs were covered to protect myself from his claws.

"Oh Biiiiing. Bingy Bing." I crept around the hall and poked my head into the lounge. Nothing. I slowly went up the stairs and into the bedroom, seeing a lump under my pillow. "Come on, Bing, come on." Nothing. I pulled out the secret weapon. "Dreamies." I gave the bag a little shake. Like a genie at the rub of a lamp, Bing appeared from under my pillow to drop next to my feet, ears pointing up and tail fluffed. I held out my hand, revealing two of his tasty treats. But Bing was not so dumb.

I stepped back with the Dreamies still in my hand, trying to tempt him my way, but he stayed put. He blinked, whiskers flared, and slowly turned around so his back was facing me. I didn't have time to mess about. I put the treats in my pocket and lunged forward, grabbing him and risking certain death by a thousand scratches by quickly shoving him in the carrier which I had relocated to the landing.

"There we go," I said, as he growled at me from his prison. "That wasn't so bad, was it?"

My car rolled down Sarah's driveway at just after twelve. I smiled at her house, admiring how far my friend had come this year. From being so broken thanks to Max the Wanker, she was now a born-again independent woman. And my friend was finally back on the dating scene and had even found someone she liked. I couldn't wait to hear all about it.

Bing grumbled from the back seat.

"Okay, okay. We're going."

I carefully coordinated myself so I could carry everything,

Bing included, to the house. I fumbled with the keys and eventually managed to bring all the belongings inside.

"Hang on in there, Bing," I reassured him. "You wait until I've got your things ready."

I pulled his dishes out first, put fresh water in one and biscuits in the other, and placed them both on the floor by the fridge. I was just about to start on his litter tray when I thought I heard creaking floorboards coming from the bedroom. I tried not to think about it. Houses make noises, especially old ones. I had asked Sarah whether it was a good idea buying such an old house, in case it came with a resident ghost.

"Not all old houses are haunted," she'd reassured me. *"Walls crack and floorboards creak, it happens."*

I wasn't entirely convinced then, and I still wasn't now. As hard as I tried to ignore the creaking and the footsteps, and whatever was approaching the door to the kitchen, my heart was pounding with fear. I grabbed the nearest object I could find to defend myself, as the door was thrown open. I winced and took a step back, readying myself to attack.

"A spatula? Really?" Sarah stepped into the kitchen and closed the door behind her. "You almost gave me a heart attack. I thought someone had broken in."

"Right back at ya, sista." I put the spatula back on the counter while my heart tried to resume its normal pace. "What are you doing here? I assumed you were at work. Your car wasn't on the drive when I arrived."

"I left it in town. I'm going to go pick it up later. We ended up having some drinks and..."

"Ah yes, the date." I looked at my friend, who was still fastening her dressing gown and flattening her hair. Or trying to, at least. That hair was a sure sign of a good night. "The bed got christened last night then?"

"Well..." It wasn't often that Sarah blushed.

"It's okay, it's okay." I held up my hands. "We're saving all the juicy gossip for when I'm back. I won't push you for details. Did you get my text?"

"No," her eyes darted to the door, wincing at the footsteps that were making their way from the bedroom, "I'll have a look though, and send you a reply. Just leave Bing's stuff there, I'll sort it all out, and I'll..."

The door opened.

There he stood.

My ex-friend-with-benefits. Dan.

CHAPTER FOURTEEN

Our eyes locked. I wasn't imagining anything. It was Dan. My Dan. My very own ex. The guy I had been having sex with, on and off, for nearly a decade. So, *he* was the guy that Sarah had been seeing. The one she liked and had been texting every day since they'd had their first date. After everything, why didn't she feel she could tell me about it? Why not be honest from the outset?

Thoughts were flying around inside my head, not making any sense. How long had they been talking? Was it when we found him on the dating app? Who made the first move? Were they falling in love? I looked down at Bing in his carrier, as he started scratching at the floor, making me remember why I was there. I released the catch on his carrier. I didn't look at Sarah. I couldn't.

I directed my comments to the cupboard door. "He's eaten already this morning. Don't let him make you think he's dying of hunger at any time. He will be lying." I picked up his bag of food and toys and placed them on Sarah's table. "His things are in there. Dreamies, too. No more than five a day, or else he'll be sick, probably in the last place you want him to be.

There's a blanket in there that might make him a bit more comfortable in a new place, he likes to sleep on it. Thank you so much."

"Jenny..." Sarah stepped towards me.

"I have to go, I have some things still to pack." I turned towards the door.

"Don't go."

"I'll call you when I'm home and arrange to pick him up. Thanks again for having him."

"Jenny..." I heard Dan's voice as I pulled the front door open and stepped outside, but I didn't stop to hear what he had to say. I kept on going, almost dropping my car keys as I fumbled with them in my pocket to get the car door open. I had to get away as quickly as I could. I was followed closely by a frantic Sarah, who grabbed my car door, preventing me from shutting it and driving away as fast as possible.

"I'm sorry," she said, tears forming in her eyes. "I was going to tell you when you got back. I didn't know where this would lead. Whether it would even lead anywhere. I wasn't sure how to tell you. We just–"

"I need to go, Sarah. We'll talk after my holiday, like we originally planned to do." I held on to the steering wheel, too scared to look at her in case I started to cry too.

"Look, I get that it's weird and I can kind of understand why you'd feel a bit jealous, but–"

"Jealous?" I cut her off. "You think I'm jealous? Sarah, Dan can do whatever the hell he likes. *You* can do what you like. You and he can do whatever you like together. You're both single adults. I don't care that you and he are together. You're both great, amazing people. If I'd liked him in *that* way, then I would have taken that step with him when *he* wanted to make it more serious."

"Then what's the problem?" Her panic switched to

confusion. It made me angrier. How could she not understand why I was so upset with her? I finally looked at her.

"The problem is, after everything we have been through, not just the last twelve months, *everything,* you couldn't pick up the phone and tell me you were going on a date with Dan."

"I didn't know how you'd react."

"And that's the problem. You didn't want to find out how I might react. You just went ahead even though you thought there was a possibility that I would be mad. *That* is the problem."

"I'm sorry." It was her turn to be at a loss for words. Dan appeared at the doorway, not saying anything. Sarah tried again. "I did a really shitty thing. I've betrayed you. Please, Jenny, can we talk?"

"I need to go. I'll see you when I get back."

Sarah stepped back and allowed me to shut the car door. I pulled away and drove off, not wanting to look at either of them.

I barely registered my brother's Tesla parked outside my house when I got back. I just reversed onto my drive without really paying attention. I was so upset and distracted that I had to do a quick check to be sure that I'd pulled onto the correct drive.

My head was spinning with thoughts by the time I got home from Sarah's. I'd needed to clear my head, so on the way home I drove to Ogden Reservoir, where I knew it would be peaceful at that time of day and I would be able to clear my head.

As I followed the trail around the water that was surrounded by trees and passed the odd dog walker who nodded in greeting, I found a sheltered bench and sat down. I tried picturing Sarah and Dan together. I had known them both for such a long time. Dan had matured over the years. From the look of his dating-app profile, he really was ready for love, and I trusted him to look after Sarah. Also, if he was going to find the right kind of girl anywhere who would be a partner as well as a best friend, it was Sarah. She had learned from her mistakes with Max The Wanker, and while her barriers might have been up with other dates, she would know what she was getting with Dan as I had spoken about him for years, so why couldn't she speak to me about him?

After a while, I wandered around the reservoir once more, and thought about all that Sarah and I had been through together, over the years. The immature boyfriends, the horrors of university hangovers, the first holiday to Zante all those years ago, and all the other trips since. We were best friends, maybe even soulmates, so why couldn't she have spoken to me first? Why couldn't she have told me they were meeting up for a date?

Zack met me in the hallway as I walked through the front door.

"Where've you been? I was getting worried." He hugged me close. "I tried calling, but you didn't answer. Are you all right?"

I could see the worry in his eyes. I could feel his heart beating fast.

"Oh, fine," I lied. "I was just making sure Bing was settled in before I left. Got his litter tray set up and all that." Great, now I was the dishonest one. On my walk, I had wondered about telling Zack why I'd had a falling out with Sarah. Would he take it the wrong way and think I was jealous about Sarah and Dan, like she had thought initially? Or would he understand that I felt betrayed? I didn't want to be a hypocrite and keep things from him. "Actually, I had a thing with Sarah..."

"Is she back? Is she still in one piece?" Andrew's voice shouted from the living room. Had Zack called in the cavalry to search for me?

"Hey," I walked into the room and found Andrew sitting

comfortably in an armchair with a brew, "what are you doing here?"

"Liz found my stash of sausage rolls in the garage and threw me out."

"What?!" I dropped my bag to the floor at his announcement. "Are you being serious? Oh, that bloody woman…"

"I'm kidding! Calm down. I have that integrated fridge in one of the units, so she'll never find out." He winked. "But if you have any bacon, I'd be up for a butty. And sausages. And burgers. Anything, just feed me something meaty so I don't call at Burger King on my way home."

Zack laughed. "The poor guy! He's lacking good, decent protein. I've got us a pepperoni pizza for tea, you're welcome to have some if you like?" he offered.

"Actually, I won't stick around much longer." Andrew checked his phone. "Liz is needing me back to help get the kids fed, bathed and in bed. But if I leave now, I'll be able to nip to Tesco and grab something to eat. Build up my strength. Cora isn't a fan of going to sleep without a fight." He rubbed his eyes and stood up.

"You never answered my question," I said. "What are you doing here?"

"Can't a big brother call in on his little sister to chew the fat? Actually, I was just passing, had a conference at a hotel in Halifax and thought I'd call in while I was over this way. Zack and I were just catching up, talking sports, debating the best way to build a fire, typical man stuff."

"Okay, okay. Go back to your mud hut and eat your homemade hummus. We'll be tucking into a meat-filled pizza as soon as you're gone."

He playfully punched my arm, and then pulled me in for a hug goodbye.

"Have a great holiday. Zack was telling me about the villa. It sounds awesome! A lot better than that place you stayed in Zante with the–"

"We don't need to go there!" I almost shouted. I knew I'd regret telling him about it when it happened, but I needed him to cover for me at the time.

"Oh, before I go, Mum told me to remind you to shave your legs. 'Tell her it's Greece, not Germany'," he said, mimicking her voice.

"Oh my God. Goodbye Andrew, it's been a pleasure."

"Ha, ha! See you soon, bud." He patted Zack on the back as I forcefully but nicely shoved him out of the door before he could say anything more to try and embarrass me.

"That was random," I said. "I can't remember the last time my brother was at my house. What was he *really* up to?"

"He was just passing after a work thing, like he said." Zack shrugged. "So, we had a chat over a coffee. Are you hungry yet? I'll go put some food in the oven. Then it's time for an early night." He kissed me on the head and made his way to the kitchen.

I pulled my phone out of my bag. There were several missed calls and a message. Quite a few were from Zack, who had been trying to find out where I was, but there was a message from Sarah too.

> Please forgive me. I did a shitty thing. You didn't deserve that. Call me. I'll always be here. The Greek word for 'tea' is 'toai' if you need to use it. Xxx

I put my phone away. I wasn't ready to call her just yet.

CHAPTER FIFTEEN

Crete was the most beautiful place I had ever seen. It had clear blue skies, even clearer seas and an air-conditioned taxi keeping us cool from the thirty-degree heat that almost melted me as I stepped off the plane. A heatwave back home was unbearable, but this felt perfect.

"This is Agios Nikolaos," Zack said with an impressive accent as we drove through a busy town. "We're nearly there now." He looked around in wonder at the place he had spent many summers when growing up.

There were streets lined with shops and restaurants. The marina was full of yachts and there was an actual cruise ship in the port too! I spied all the touristy shops full of knick-knacks and tat. I loved those shops. They all sold the same stuff for the same price, but I still always felt the need to go in and buy something I would never buy at home. Like a ceramic Hercules, which I am sure every Cretan has in their home. I would need a mini statue of a Greek god to take home with me. If anything, purely because my mum would hate it. I wondered whether they might have one of Medusa that I could gift her.

"Could we come back and do some shopping?" I asked.

"Of course! We can do whatever we like. We have two whole weeks here." He reached for my hand. "There will be plenty of time for shopping, exploring, sunbathing, relaxing. Anything you want."

The taxi wove down narrow roads and out of the town. We passed huge five-star hotels and eventually made our way down a long driveway with a few villas dotted about. They were all painted white, with blue shutters on every window, and perfect manicured lawns out front with Greek pots decorating the doorways. All I could think was that 'villa' was a very modest term for these mansions, although I did not say that to Zack.

"And we're here!" Zack squeezed my hand before getting out of the taxi. The driver was already at the boot getting our cases out for us.

"Hello, travellers!" Alistair came out of the palace before us, looking tiny in comparison to it, with his arms open wide to greet us. "How was the flight? Was there a long wait for your suitcases? I do hope there wasn't any traffic. Oh, let me pay for the taxi." He finally stopped to take a breath, whilst moving his sunglasses to the top of his pink head as he pulled his wallet from his pocket.

"Where's Mum?" Zack asked.

"She's just having a siesta." He handed some money to the driver. "She's been out in the garden all morning, seeing to the flowers. Tired the poor old girl out." He picked up my suitcase once the taxi pulled away. "Don't tell her I called her that." He winked and led us both inside.

The entrance hall could have been a room on its own. In fact, I initially thought I was walking into the sitting room, as there were two large sofas as well as a coffee table. He took us to the bottom of the stairs in the far corner and plonked down my case.

"I'll let Zack give you the official tour, I have to get back to

Stan. He's got the football on at his place and, whilst the ladies are having their afternoon naps, we aren't getting any complaints." He chuckled. "I will see you two kids later on."

He put his sunglasses back on and sauntered through another door and out of sight.

"Who's Stan?"

"Stan and Beverley, my parents' friends who own the villa next door. They'll be here with their daughter, Chloe." Ah yes, the twenty-something who would be living next door to us for a fortnight. Marvellous. Zack picked up our suitcases. "Come on, I'll race you upstairs."

"Woah," I laughed, "slow down, you cheater! You know where we're going, I don't." I grabbed his arm. "Won't we wake your mum?" I didn't want to annoy her on my first day there.

"Not a chance, their room is in the opposite direction to ours."

Looking up to the landing, I felt like I was in *Downton Abbey*. I don't think I could even call it a landing. It was more like a gallery, with a huge window in the tall ceiling, allowing the sun to beam down the stairs. I followed my giddy boyfriend to the top and then down the corridor and through a door.

"Well, this just won't do." I followed him in and shook my head at the ridiculously large room. "It's not even remotely big enough for the two of us." I sat on the king-size bed, looking up to the double doors which led out to a balcony. There were two double wardrobes, a grey patterned chair in the corner next to a desk, and some shelves filled with books. If I were to wear a pedometer and walk once around the room, I was pretty sure I would have hit the recommended daily step count.

"Not big enough for you, m'lady?"

"Nope, sorry, you'll need to sleep somewhere else. We can't possibly both fit in here. I have standards, don't you know?"

He put the cases down in front of the wardrobes and made

his way to join me on the bed, pushing me so I was lying on my back, and climbing on top of me.

"You would kick me out of my own room?" He nuzzled at my neck, kissing me in the right places.

"Absolutely. You'd need to sleep in the servants' quarters."

"I'll be right back." He kissed me once more, and then bounced back off the bed and through another door.

"Where does that door lead to? Cinema? Recording studio?"

"Just our own private bathroom, nothing that exciting." He smiled and closed the door behind him. There was even an en suite. I may never be persuaded to leave this place.

I got up and walked to the double doors. Clicking the latch, I slid them open and let the sun hit my face for a moment. It didn't feel as uncomfortable as Rome had. The heat was different here somehow. In Rome, I knew I would be walking around for hours and hours in the heat, but here, there was a pool at my disposal and an ocean not too far away.

Stepping forward, I walked out onto the balcony and viewed the surroundings. I could see a few villas dotted around. There was no one else about, so maybe everyone was having an afternoon snooze. I glanced down at the pool and smiled to myself. It didn't matter that it was shared with Alistair and Miranda's friends, it was still private. We wouldn't need to compete with other families or children wanting to splash about. Also, it was huge, and there were a dozen sun loungers around it as well as couches and umbrellas for shade. I could see the outdoor kitchen area with a large dining table just visible under a canopy. I was in heaven. Maybe I could be brave and wear one of my bikinis later on, to top up my tan.

Then again.

Maybe I won't.

My eyes nearly fell out of my head as I spotted the girl I

assumed was Chloe the neighbours' daughter. The twenty-something. A twenty-something with the body of a Victoria's Secret model, and breasts perky enough to poke your eye out, clearly displayed in her barely-there bikini. I'm only thirty-one, and I've never had children, but I still felt like I should be wearing a burkini instead of a bikini, for decency. This was supposed to be a relaxing holiday, now I'd feel like I was competing with her. I couldn't possibly do that.

Two arms came from behind and pulled me close.

"Enjoying the view?" Zack asked.

Not as much as he probably was. How many summers had he spent here with her looking like that? There was almost a ten-year age gap, but still, summer loving and all that.

"It's amazing." I looked back up to the actual scenery. "Although I'm disappointed I can't see the sea from here. As well as the tiny bedroom to put up with, it's not to my taste. I won't be leaving a good review on Tripadvisor."

"The sea is on the other side." His hands were wandering now. "I'll show you later. We can even have a wander down to the beach once we've eaten, and watch the sunset, if you're not too tired. It should be cooler by then too."

"Is that Chloe?" I had to ask. Probably not my smartest move, alerting his eyes to that whilst he fondled my body.

"It is." He glanced down for a second to check, before returning his attention to me.

"Does she always dress like that?"

"Only when her parents aren't looking, they're quite conservative. Especially her mum. You'll like Chloe though, she's a lot of fun." His hand found my bra, which he undid in record time. "Come on, let's get you unpacked."

～

"We are so glad you're here!" Miranda said, clinking my glass of wine against hers. Alistair had just cooked a delicious meal. I was conscious of trying not to eat too much, worried I would gain too much weight, but the more wine Zack's mum poured for me, the less I cared.

"It is such a beautiful house!" I exclaimed. "I swear, I almost got lost when I nipped up to the bathroom."

Zack and his parents laughed. He held my hand. It was strange to see him in a different environment. It was usually just us, and I loved that it was just us. I was seeing a completely different side to him when he was with his family though, and it made me love him even more.

"I just wish I'd been awake to greet you." She playfully slapped her husband's arm. "You should have woken me up."

"Oh, I know better than that, my love." He leaned forward and kissed her cheek.

"Don't worry, it's fine, Zack had to give me a tour anyway." And see that I was sufficiently satisfied atop every piece of furniture in our room.

"Well," she gulped the last of her wine, her eyelids seeming heavy, "I think we'll leave you kids to it for a few days. Let you enjoy yourselves without us old fuddy-duddies. We won't get in your way. Do what you like, but we will be having a big meal here one night this week along with next door, so I hope you'll join us for that."

"Of course." I grinned. I loved Miranda. If this were my mother, she would have a military-planned itinerary for us, with a different excursion every day and a very strict schedule to keep. There would be no chance of any alone time. "We can help out."

"Not at all. Once that barbeque is lit, Beverley and I are banished from the cooking area. All we need to do is pick out the wine."

"That seems like a serious job, I am willing to help," I happily offered.

"I'm glad to hear it." She squeezed my arm. I wanted her to adopt me.

"Well, my dear," Alistair piped up, placing his empty glass on the table, "that's today's wine allowance used up. Shall we call it a night?"

"I think we should."

We all stood up to say goodnight to each other, with more hugs. I loved this family. I began clearing away the plates, but Miranda stopped me, telling us both to enjoy our first evening and to leave the used plates and glasses out to be cleaned away in the morning.

"Fancy a skinny-dip?" Zack whispered, as soon as his parents were out of earshot.

"What's gotten into you?" I blushed. "You're never usually this daring. How much wine have you had?"

"Not a lot, I hate the stuff. Come on, no one will see. Their room faces the other side."

And so, filled up on expensive wine, I stripped down to my birthday suit and my thirty-one-year-old boobs and I joined my naked boyfriend for a quick dip in the pool.

By the time we climbed into bed shortly afterwards, I knew I was ready for a long and deep sleep. I checked my phone first, and there was a message from Sarah. No words, just a photo of Bing, curled up asleep in her new armchair, looking quite at home. Zack got in next to me and I showed him the message.

"Have you spoken to her yet?"

"No." I put my phone on the side table and laid down, sinking into the pillows.

"Just let things cool down whilst you're here. Try and talk to her when we get home. Best to do it face to face anyway."

I realise I'll have to talk to her at some point. After all, she does have my cat in her care. But what on earth would I say to her? Do I apologise for storming out? Is she in the wrong? I don't need to think about it yet. I have two weeks of living in paradise ahead of me. My relationship with Sarah is a problem for another time.

It was a relief to tell Zack about it on the plane. Luckily, he understood why I was so upset, and didn't feel worried that I might still have had feelings for Dan. He said it would all blow over soon enough. I did hope so. I needed to brag that I'd just swam naked in my boyfriend's parents' pool and had sex on a sun lounger, and there was only one person in my life who would appreciate such gossip.

CHAPTER SIXTEEN

Zack had asked if I wanted to visit the local town after breakfast. It seemed like a great idea – it looked lovely as we drove through it yesterday – however, it turned out to have been a very bad idea walking the short distance into Agios Nikolaos. The sun was hot, hot, hot and my feet were now dead, dead, dead. My trusty little handheld fan was now clinging on for life, but doing a good job keeping a constant breeze on my face, but my poor feet would need a cool soak later on. Or right this second.

"I should have worn my trainers," I said. You'd have thought I'd have learned after Rome. Sandals are not for walking long distances.

"We can get a taxi to take us back when we're done," he promised. "And I'll give you a foot massage too, how does that sound?"

"Sounds perfect." I smiled. I let go of his hand and slipped my arm around his back, and he did the same to me. Affectionate, yes, but it also meant I could lean on him a bit. I didn't want to kick off this fantastic holiday by moaning. My poor feet though...

Once in the centre of the town, we walked over a small bridge, which ran over a sliver of sea. The bridge led to a small lake, which had bars and restaurants circled around it and was overlooked by a rocky hillside with various random religious shapes carved into it. And cats. Lots of cats that were clearly feral, yet seemed much friendlier than my pampered Bing.

As I looked out over the edge of the water, I could just make out large groups of fish sitting under the shade of the bridge, almost teasing me to join them where it was nice and cool. It was only ten o'clock in the morning, but it was scorching. I was pleased I'd chosen to wear factor-fifty suncream for the first day of the trip. I looked further into the small lake, but I couldn't see the bottom. Although the sea itself was turquoise, this small body of water was almost black. We called into one of the restaurants for a drink and the waiter told us how locals believed the lake to be bottomless. Apparently, it was said that one of the Greek goddesses used to bathe in it at night.

We rehydrated ourselves, sipping on freshly squeezed orange juice, and rested our feet before setting off again and taking in more of the town. We walked hand in hand as we admired the small independent shops. One of the shops actually led down into a cave, where a little old Greek man was selling his handmade wooden souvenirs. He sat in the corner, chiselling away as we browsed. I fell in love with the shops selling handmade jewellery. Zack told me to pick something out so he could treat me, but I couldn't make up my mind.

"There's no rush," he said, with his arm around me. "We have loads of time here yet."

We set off again and held hands as we walked past the cruise ship stationed at the marina, a different one to yesterday. Around the coastline, all I could see was blue. It was difficult to see where the sky ended and the sea began. I could understand why Zack's parents would want their holiday home to be there. It was wonderful.

"Let me know when you're hungry," Zack said as we sat on a bench watching a man sitting with his legs dangling off the pier, a bucket on one side of him and bait on the other as he firmly held his fishing rod. "We can find somewhere to eat. You have a lot of places to pick from."

"I know where I want to eat," I said confidently, still watching the fisherman.

"If you're waiting for Achilles to snag a fish, you could be waiting a while." Our Greek fisherman was not having much luck.

"Dammit. Well, my second option was back near the lake. Did you see the restaurant that sits on the sea edge? It looked good."

"I've been there, you'll love the pizzas." He stood up and pulled me up with him. "I've been there a few times with Chloe. She and her parents don't get on very well, and whenever they pushed her a bit too far, we'd escape down here and grab a bite there. It's a great place."

I felt a pang of jealousy hit me right in the gut. I'd not met her yet, and already I was beginning to hate her. I just needed to keep reminding myself that he brought *me* here with him. Even though he knew she would be here, and he could have left me at home, he brought me. I needed to stop being silly. This wasn't the same as Sarah's situation with Max The Wanker.

It was just after twelve o'clock when we arrived at the restaurant, just in time for lunch. The tables were sheltered with a huge canopy so we could enjoy our food without feeling like we were on a grill. There were fans scattered about too, blowing cool air from the sea breeze onto us, which was nice.

We both ordered iced water and asked for a few minutes to look over the menu. I looked up at Zack sitting across from me.

He was reading his menu, but glanced up and gave me his mischievous grin.

"What are you thinking?" I flirted with him, tickling his leg with my foot.

"I'm wondering if we could get the pool to ourselves again tonight."

"What did you have in mind, specifically?" I leaned in closer, not wanting the neighbouring tables to hear us.

"Well," Zack closed his menu and put his hands on mine, bringing his face close to me, "I thought we could…"

"Oh my God, Zack! Aahhh!" The unmistakeable mating call of a twenty-something girl erupted from behind us, shocking one of the waiters, who almost stumbled over the edge of the pier and into the sea. He survived, but the bundle of clean tablecloths he was carrying did not.

We both looked up and saw Chloe bounding towards us, her abs on show for the whole of the island to see. Zack was barely able to stand up before she threw her arms around him, her long hair flinging over his shoulders as though claiming its territory. She was one of those girls who, like Sarah, could allow her hair to flow freely no matter how hot and sticky the weather was. I subconsciously made sure my ponytail was still in place, and that my top was pulled down over my stomach.

Zack pulled back from her grasp. "It's great to see you. What are you doing here at this time? I didn't think you kids liked to get up before noon."

"Oh, my mum was driving me up the wall." She pulled back the chair next to Zack, put her shopping bags under the table, and sat down. "She was going on and on about me going back to uni and finishing my law degree. I had to get out." She turned to me and elbowed Zack in the side. "Are you going to introduce us then? Men!" She tutted and laughed. "They're so rude, aren't they? Do you know I saw the funniest TikTok today about a female Greek poet called Sappho who was married to a man called Kerkylas of Andros, which actually translates to Dick Allcocks from Man Island, isn't that hilarious?" She shrieked again. "So fitting sometimes. Not that you're a dick, Zack, you know I love you." She stroked his arm. "So, introduce us!"

As Zack made an official introduction, I outstretched my hand, but she got up from her seat and smothered me with a hug. "It is so nice to meet you!" She returned to the seat next to Zack. "It's so nice to finally have a girl here too. Not that Zack isn't fun, with the amount of late-night pool parties we've had over the years." She playfully elbowed him in the ribs. "Has he made you his signature piña colada yet? He makes such a good cocktail." She rubbed his arm again. "We got so wasted last year, do you remember?"

"Vaguely." He laughed, looking uncomfortable.

"My mum was so mad, as we'd used all the rum. Hilarious. It was worth the scolding." It was difficult to keep up with her. I'd never heard anyone speak so fast and without stopping for breath before.

They seemed so comfortable in each other's company, which was nice, but the idea of them getting drunk and having a pool party of their own made me lose my appetite, even if it was in the past. I had a niggling urge to call Sarah. I needed her to tell me it was all okay and there was no reason to worry.

"Have you ordered yet?" She picked up Zack's menu. "I'm starving."

"We were just looking over the menu. Have you decided yet?" He reached out for my hand, pulling me towards him, and out of my nightmare daze.

"Oh, sorry, no. Well, actually–"

"We should get a pizza," Chloe cut in. "Get the massive one and share it. It'll be enough for the three of us, it was too much for just us two last year, but I reckon we can manage."

"Let's do it, we're on holiday." Zack put his menu down and called the waiter over, ordering the large pepperoni pizza. At least he had picked my favourite topping.

An hour later, I should have been in total bliss. Perfect pizza, sexy boyfriend opposite me, the never-ending ocean to my right, but unfortunately there was something on our table demanding all of the attention. If I had a shot of ouzo for every time she rubbed his arm, I would have been mighty tipsy. Why couldn't she just back off? I got that they'd known each other for a long time, but you don't constantly touch someone's boyfriend right in front of them. Was she jealous that he was with another woman?

"Well, I should go," Chloe finally said, standing up. "Do you want any money for the pizza?" She put her hand on Zack's shoulder and I fought every urge not to push her into the sea.

"Nah, don't worry about it. You can get the next one."

"Okay, laters!" She felt the need to bend down, arse so close to Zack's face he could have kissed it, to pick up her bags from the floor and finally leave us alone. So much for a romantic lunch, all I could picture now were her perfect buttocks and thighs. She didn't need to worry about chafing in this heat.

"Sorry about Chloe, she can be a bit much sometimes. Are you all right?" he asked. "You've been quite quiet."

"Oh yeah, it's pretty hot. I can get grumpy if I'm too hot, sorry." It was broadly true, I did get grumpy when too hot, but it was a lie right now. This was supposed to be a relaxing holiday, a first holiday, with my boyfriend. How could I relax if Chloe was going to pop up unexpectedly at any moment?

"Well, let's head back up to the villa. We can get a taxi and have a siesta in our air-conditioned bedroom once we're back." Now it was his turn to tease *my* leg with his foot. He rubbed my hand with his finger, up my arm to my face, pulling me close as he leaned over the table to kiss me. "I am sorry about Chloe though, she is used to being the centre of attention. She properly monopolised our lunch there."

"Just a bit. Not to mention talking non-stop about you two having had mad summer pool parties."

"Not like our pool party last night, please don't think that. She's not interested in me. We've been friends for a long time, ever since our parents bought those villas."

The waiter came by with our bill and Zack pulled out some money.

"I don't mind if you want to walk back up," I lied. "Save money on a taxi."

"In this heat at this time of day? Neither of us will survive. Come on," he grabbed my hand, pulling me up with him, "our bath is big enough for the two of us. No one can interrupt us there, and your feet need a good rub."

On the third day of our holiday, we had managed to get the villa all to ourselves. Alistair and Miranda had gone out to meet friends and wouldn't be back until that night. Stan, Beverley and Chloe were also absent for the day, which meant the pool was ours for the taking. As the pool was private for just the two villas, and was away from public view, it meant no one could see us as we fooled around under the water. Pool sex was an odd but welcome experience. I couldn't wait to tell Sarah about it. Well, if I would be telling her at all. She would love how we'd attempted it on a lilo though. I'm not sure why we thought that would work, however, that is how we ended up underwater.

"What time is everyone due back?" I asked, as I wrapped myself in a towel and positioned myself on a sun lounger under an umbrella. It was mid-afternoon and nearing thirty degrees. Definitely time for an afternoon nap in some shade.

"I don't know." He pulled one of the loungers up next to mine so we could lie together. "Later on tonight, I think. They won't be rushing back. Do you want a drink before we snuggle up?" He had been so attentive all day. Whether it was to make me feel better for the meal yesterday, I wasn't sure. Or was this just who he always was? Every night before bed, he always asked me if I wanted a drink, or anything to eat. The other week, just as we had been falling asleep, I realised I had left my phone in the living room. I use my phone for my morning alarm, so shoved the duvet off myself ready to go and get it, but Zack went instead, instructing me to stay comfortable. That's just who he was.

"I'm all right, thanks. I've got a bottle of water somewhere." I pulled my sunglasses down over my eyes. I was finally feeling like I was on holiday. Our skin was still wet from the pool, so the breeze felt nice on my skin. "This is so comfy. Can we stay here forever?"

"You won't get any argument from me. This is heaven."

A gentle breeze blew over us. A cicada called out from somewhere in the grass. Zack's breathing got heavier next to me as he began to fall asleep. Otherwise, the silence filled my ears, and I was soon joining Zack in the land of nod.

I was lost in the villa. Each door led me back to the entrance. How do I get out? I could hear laughter through the door to my right. I pushed it open, expecting to be in the dining room, but I found I was back in the entrance. I ran up the flight of stairs and through our bedroom door, but I was back in the entrance again. Help!

"Zack!" I called out. "Where are you? Help!"

"I'm through here!" He laughed, as he shouted from the next room.

I ran forward, pushing the door open, expecting to be back where I started, but I could see the back of the sofa. Finally, I was no longer trapped in a labyrinth. Zack's head was visible, so I walked around to join him, but he was sitting with Chloe. No, he was lain on top of her on the sofa. They were cuddling, kissing...

"What's going on?" I shouted. "What are you doing?"

I woke myself up by calling out in my sleep. Zack sat up and shuffled closer to me.

"Are you all right? You jumped pretty hard there. Bad dream?"

"Something like that." My mind shot back to visions of Chloe and Zack kissing in my dream. As I woke up fully, I released my clenched jaw and breathed out. My towel had slipped down, exposing rather too much of my cleavage. I was brave enough to wear a bikini today knowing we would be all alone, but I had started to feel very insecure since my dream. "What time is it?" I removed my sunglasses, feeling where they had dug into the side of my head and left an imprint.

"Woah, almost four. We've slept for a while." He yawned as he sat up and stretched. "Oh, hello! When did *you* get here?"

I looked up to see who he was talking to nearby, hoping his parents hadn't witnessed my boob slippage.

"I've been here ages. You two were well out of it!" Chloe was on the sun lounger opposite us, lying on her front next to a discarded bikini top, evidently topless. "You were making some funny noises, Jenny." She giggled.

"I thought you were out all day?" Zack rubbed his eyes.

"Nah, I couldn't be bothered spending the whole day with *them* two. I slept in late and was going to come out here, but saw you two were busy enjoying yourselves earlier." She winked. I was mortified. "So, I hid inside until you fell asleep and then I came out. Actually," she sat up, pulling her top across her front, "Zack, could you top up the suncream on my back for me? I don't think I got it everywhere, and I'd hate to burn."

"Of course." I watched as he sat behind her, rubbing factor

ten into her neck and shoulders. I mean, come on. Factor ten? Why bother? You may as well rub milk into your skin. Why was she doing this? What about girl code? I think the most touchy-feely I ever got with Max The Wanker was when he accidentally stood on Bing's tail, after which his leg looked like it'd had an encounter with Freddy Krueger, so I helped to clean him up with antiseptic wipes.

I pulled my towel over myself and stood up.

Chloe glanced up, just for long enough to flutter her eyelashes and give me a half smile.

"Where are you going, babe?" Zack asked, continuing to rub the suncream onto her shoulders.

"Just nipping to the bathroom, won't be a tick."

As soon as I got inside, I ran up the stairs, holding back tears. In our room, I found my phone, which I'd left on charge. There was another photo from Sarah with a message. This time, Bing was in her kitchen, sprawled on his back in a seemingly mischievous mood.

> Your cat somehow found my favourite red, lacy
> thong, mistaking it for cat food, and ate it…
> He's okay. The thong, however, met a grim
> end. X

I laughed out loud, tears filling my eyes. My finger hovered over the 'call' button, but I hesitated. I didn't want to break our silence with my tears over a silly bit of jealousy, although if someone was going to understand my concerns about a twenty-something girl, it would be Sarah. I peeked out of the window at Zack and Chloe. They were laughing together, their heads close. She playfully pushed him. In my mind I was 'playfully' pushing her too. Towards the deep end of the pool.

CHAPTER SEVENTEEN

"*A*nd so, I told the shop assistant, if she did not know the origin of avocado, she did not deserve to have employment in a delicatessen." Beverley finished her sixth glass of wine. "I mean, honestly. I told her manager she would be better suited to a budget store."

"I'm sorry about my mum." Chloe leaned closer to me, whispering, "Complete snob. She acts like a work coach for the elite, but has never worked a bloody day in her life."

I had to laugh. We were halfway through the first week of our holiday and Miranda had asked us to join them all for a group meal with the neighbours. I had been feeling awkward around Zack, wondering whether I should bring up my concerns about Chloe, and their behaviour. It didn't feel right. They had known each other for a long time. Longer than I had known him. I had always been on the side of men and women being friends, without it meaning anything. I had always managed it myself, and been fine with other partners' female friendships, but this one was really bothering me.

If I were to bring it up, would it cause our first major argument? I didn't want a fall-out with him as well as with my best friend. That was too much emotion to handle at once. I know Sarah was bitter at the time, going through that awful break-up herself, but maybe some part of her theory about twenty-somethings stuck with me, and that was why I was being so cautious. Did I have a reason to be threatened by Chloe?

She was a completely different person tonight. There was very little flesh on show, although Zack had told me that her parents were quite conservative, so it was probably for their benefit that she was covered up. She was quite reserved, only sipping her wine, and spent most of the dinner making an effort to try to get to know me. I had to admire her for it.

"Zack was telling me all about your cat," she said. "I'd love a cat, but Daddy is allergic. Did Bing really leave a dead mouse in your toilet?"

"Oh my God, yes he did. I couldn't even bring myself to scoop it out until I was elbow-deep in several pairs of Marigolds so there was no chance of it touching me."

"And the spiders?" She laughed. "Does he really leave them in your shoes?"

"He hasn't done that for a while." I recoiled at the memory. "But when he was younger, it was his favourite game."

"That's hilarious." She sipped her wine. "You should write a blog or something. Like on *Marley and Me*. Maybe 'The World of Bing', or 'Bing Things'."

We laughed together, like we were besties on a night out. Her parents were snobs, but she was clearly the complete opposite, and we sniggered like schoolgirls every time her mother shared another First World problem. She was actually being really friendly. I decided to stop being such a tit. She was young and probably didn't understand the concept of boundaries with guys with their girlfriends. I know I didn't care at that age, so why should she? Plus, she clearly enjoyed the attention. Was that really a crime? I knew that Zack and I had a secure relationship, and were deeply in love. I decided not to let it bother me anymore.

"And they ran out of hummus!" Beverley's voice overpowered the table once again. "This is the twenty-first century. How can there be a hummus shortage?"

"It was probably my sister-in-law," I whispered to Zack and Chloe. "Stocking up for winter."

He hid his laugh behind his bottle of Becks, longing, like the rest of us, for this painful yet hilarious night to come to an end.

"Well, Beverley, maybe you should start ordering online," Alistair piped up. He had been quiet all night, but not out of choice. Once Beverley had started complaining about trivial matters, she couldn't seem to stop. I looked at Miranda then, who caught my eye. She mouthed "I'm sorry!" to me, whilst looking very embarrassed.

"Pfft, online, have you heard him?" Beverley nudged Miranda. "Mr Techno. Once you put in your bank account details, what's to stop them taking all of your money? Those, those, what are they called?"

"Hackers?" Alistair suggested, with a sigh.

"Yes, hackers. They take it all and leave you with cookies!"

I could see Zack resisting the urge to correct her, deciding it might be more peaceful to just let her go on until she ran out of words.

"What do you kids have planned for the rest of this week then?" Miranda asked us, desperate to change the topic of conversation. "I hope you'll find time to come shopping with me, Jenny. Zack mentioned you loved all the little shops in town. Men don't appreciate shopping, so if you fancied a girly trip, I hoped you might come with me."

"I'd love to, that would be great."

"Wonderful, have you got anything booked over the next few days?"

"No, I don't think so."

"Great, we can go tomorrow or the day after. Whenever you fancy it." Miranda smiled.

"I was thinking about taking Jenny to Spinalonga tomorrow. I've been looking online and there are some tickets available," Zack said. "She can't come to Crete without seeing a bit of local history. Although, Beverley has me worried I'll be attacked by the Cookie Monster now, if I attempt to book online."

The table erupted with laughter and Chloe inadvertently spat a mouthful of wine across the table, which reached Beverley's arm.

"Chloe!" Beverley snapped. "Clean this up immediately, you're embarrassing yourself." She used her napkin to wipe her arms, while the smile disappeared from Chloe's face.

"I didn't mean to. I had a mouthful of wine and Zack made me laugh."

"You two are always messing about, one way or another. At least *he* has settled down with a nice girl. What are *you* doing with yourself these days?"

"Beverley..." Stan tried to calm his wife, but it didn't work. She was too drunk to listen to anyone. Miranda and Alistair shuffled uncomfortably in their seats as though they knew what was coming.

"Gallivanting here and there, ringing your dad for money because you've lost your bank card down some ravine in the remote islands of wherever. It's about time you sorted yourself out. Get your law degree and grow up!"

I looked over at Chloe, whose face was now beetroot. I felt such sympathy for this girl who, up until now, I had started to hate. Really, she and I had a lot in common. I thought of my own mother, who often spoke down to me when I was that age, although it was never in a drunken rage. As I got older, I learned to take my mother's harsh words with a pinch of salt, with the occasional sarcastic reply, or by not replying to her messages. My mother had wanted me to study business at university, but I chose English instead. Had I not chosen that subject, I never would have met Sarah.

I was relieved when Stan finally managed to convince Beverley to return to their villa. Miranda and Alistair decided it would be best if they called it a night too, but not before they apologised to me for their friend's drunken outburst, mindful that Chloe was still there, and not wanting to upset her even more. Miranda gave her a hug before going inside.

"Sorry about my mum," Chloe said, when it was finally just the three of us. "She gets a serious case of Bitchitus when she's had too much to drink... which is quite often."

"Are you all right?" Zack asked her.

"Yeah. Excuse me for a moment, will you? I'll be right back." She walked over to her villa and quietly slipped inside through the back door.

I turned to Zack. "That dinner took a mighty turn very quickly."

"Beverley can get like that. I think my mum hoped having you here would mean she would watch her mouth and her behaviour. She'll be absolutely mortified that all happened in front of you. Beverley is pretty great when she's sober, but once she's had a drink, you can bet money she will pick on Chloe one way or another. The thing is, she doesn't even know what's going on."

"What do you mean?"

"Chloe did go back to uni, but not to study law." He was whispering now. He leaned closer so I could hear. "She's been doing a journalism degree remotely. She does travel around a lot with friends, spends a lot of time here too, but she's been able to study at the same time and do her assignments in private. A lot of the tutorials are online now, so she can log in anywhere. You can book Zoom meetings with tutors if you need to speak to them. I know she comes across as quite immature, but she has a good head on her shoulders. Her dad knows that she's doing journalism and sends her money every now and then when she needs it. She graduates next month, but she's only invited her dad. She's adamant that her mum will *not* be there."

"So, her mum has no idea that she's about to graduate? That's awful. I thought *my* mum was bad, but she's a fairy godmother in comparison. Saying that, I don't think I'd choose to spend my summer holidays with her in such close quarters." Even if the villas were the size of a small cruise ship. "Why would she want to come with them?"

"Because–"

"Anyone up for some of this?" Chloe reappeared at the table, with a bottle of raspberry-flavoured gin and three clean glasses, so Zack stopped mid-sentence.

I really wasn't up for any more drinking. I had wanted an early night with Zack, but I didn't want to be the boring old one.

"Maybe a couple," Zack said. "But then bed, I'm shattered. And I can book us those tickets for Spinalonga tomorrow, if you like?" he said, turning to me.

"Yeah, definitely, what is it?" I asked.

"You'll find out tomorrow, but everyone needs to visit when they come here."

I yawned. We'd had quite a long day. Zack took me on a walk down to the beach after breakfast. We'd paddled, cooling our feet in the sea, before enjoying a light lunch in a small, family-run café. The beach was filled with loved-up couples, not a child in sight. One of the major benefits of going on holiday during term time.

"I'll be back in a minute," I said. "I just want to top up on after-sun. My shoulders are tingling a bit."

"Do you want a hand?" Zack tugged on my arm playfully,

pulling me down for a kiss.

"I'll be fine, you two get started."

I had left the after-sun in our bathroom after my shower earlier. Zack had smothered me in the stuff, hoping for some afternoon attention, I think, but my skin had felt too hot for bodily contact at that moment.

Up in the bathroom, I found the after-sun bottle and carefully rubbed some into my shoulders, which were feeling tender. Borrowing Chloe's factor ten had been a mistake. I would be back on the fifty tomorrow like a sensible millennial.

I could hear music playing outside, so I had a little peek out of the bathroom window. Zack and Chloe had relocated from the dining table to the sun loungers and were sitting very close together. He was whispering something in her ear. A big smile appeared on her face before she shrieked, flinging out her arms and hugging him, pushing him so hard they ended up lying back on the seat, with her on top of him.

I felt sick. I was actually going to throw up.

What had he said to her to make her so giddy? Why did she feel the need to throw herself at him and lie on top of him? Were they both insane? Or were my feelings just completely irrelevant?

I had to do it. It was either now or never.

"Hello?" It took a while for her to speak when she answered the phone, and Sarah's voice sounded uncertain.

"Hi." Unable to hide my emotion, I cried down the phone. "Are you busy? I know things have been weird with us at the moment, but I needed to talk to you."

"What's happened? Are you all right? We'll talk about *that* another time, it's paused for now. Talk to me. What's going on?"

"It's Zack. I don't know what's going on. One minute we're all loved up and it's great..." I stopped to take a breath. "I'm seriously having the best time with him. It's so beautiful here, you won't believe it. But there's this girl here. This family friend, a twenty-something, super hot girl he's known forever and she's all over him. I thought it was just one-sided, but he doesn't do anything to stop it. And just now, from the upstairs window, I watched them all over each other in a private conversation, then she ended up jumping on top of him."

"She what?! How could he do that to you? Did he push her away?" I could hear by her voice that she was furious.

"I don't know. I figured she was just an attention-seeker seeing as she's younger, but he's clearly loving it. And she is *always* there. We went for a nice lunch in town, she was there. We had some naughty pool antics, she was watching. We had the villa all to ourselves for the day, so relaxed by the pool, she was there. And now, after she's practically been my best friend all night, she's all over my boyfriend once my back is turned. I don't know what to do."

"Have you spoke to him? Found out what's going on? You need to tell Zack that you're upset." I had missed her voice. "It could be absolutely nothing to worry about. You could just ask him to be better with boundaries, without hurting her feelings. He needs to know this is bothering you."

"I will, tomorrow. Ah, although he's taking me out for the day tomorrow, somewhere called Spinny Blonga or something. He's really looking forward to showing me around. I can't do it then."

"If he's making plans for you to have the best time together, I can't see that the issue is with him. Talk to him, please."

"I will. I think I'm just going to go to bed for now. I can talk to him tomorrow evening or something. I don't want to ruin a day trip."

There was silence between us.

"How's Bing doing?" I finally asked.

"He attacked and successfully killed my laundry basket

today. And now I'm missing a bra."

"Glad to hear he's settled in quickly."

"You were up early. How are you feeling this morning?" Zack joined me at the breakfast counter, where I was picking at a croissant. "Have you still got a migraine?" He put his arm around me and kissed me on the head. When he'd finally came up to bed last night, he'd snuggled up to me and asked if I was okay. I'd told him I'd felt a headache coming on and fell asleep without meaning to.

"No, it's not too bad this morning, I'm glad I avoided the gin though. Did you guys have a fun night after I left?"

"Yeah, Chloe is mental. I'm too old for shots now. I feel like such an old man next to her." He helped himself to some coffee. "Is it too much sun, do you think? With your headache? Your shoulders looked pretty burned yesterday, maybe the walk on the beach was a bad idea. And there was me trying to be romantic, ha."

I tried to laugh with him, but it wasn't convincing.

"The walk on the beach was very romantic. It's so beautiful here."

"I'm glad I could bring you." He sat on the stool beside me. "This place means a lot to me. I wanted to share it with you."

He was being completely normal with me. Perhaps I was taking this Chloe business the wrong way. Sarah was right, I just needed to speak to him. Maybe he could have a word with Chloe and tell her to stop being so touchy-feely with him.

"I'm glad you brought me." I smiled. "I love it here."

"Are you sure you're up for today though? We could go another time. It's quite a drive up to the port, and then a quick boat ride across to the island."

I sat up. "It's an island?"

"Yeah, a very small one, but I think you'll enjoy it. There are tour guides there who take you around. They leave every hour, so if we time it right, we can join one of them. It's quite exposed to the sun though. Do you still want to go? I don't want your shoulders burning any more than they have done already."

"Absolutely, I want to go." I grinned. "I have a white blouse I can wear so I'll be covered up. Is it just going to be us two?"

"Of course it is," he assured me. "Who else would I invite?"

"I can't believe that was still a leper colony not that long ago," I said as we sat at the port of Spinalonga, waiting for our boat back across to the main island.

"I know. I've been over here a few times and it still amazes me."

We had managed to find some shade as we waited for our boat back, and had a clear view of the medieval fortress. It seemed small, but I felt as though we'd been walking around it for hours. My trainers had finally seen some use. I was glad I'd worn my white blouse. Whenever there was a breeze, it flapped around a bit, allowing some cool air to circulate and provide some relief for my shoulders. Miranda had insisted I took her sun hat too, which I'm glad I did, as we were very exposed to the sun on the tour. The guide showed us around everything from the old houses to the church.

"Thank you for bringing me." I linked his arm in mine and leaned my head on his shoulder.

"You're welcome." He kissed the top of my head. "Are you hungry? We can get some food in Elounda if you like, when the boat drops us off. There are some nice little bistros dotted about."

"That sounds good, but please let me pay," I insisted. "I haven't paid for anything yet and I feel bad. I owe you."

"This holiday was my idea." He laughed. "You don't need to pay for anything."

"I want to, though, please. Or else my mother's voice in my internal monologue will accuse me of freeloading."

"Ha! Okay, fine, the food is on you. But we're heading into Agios Nikolaos at some point so that I can buy you something. A trinket, a keepsake. You need something to remember this trip by, and I know how you love a gift shop."

A man at the port called out.

"Oh, that's our boat, come on." Zack stood and pulled me up. "If we get on first, we can get to the side with the shade... Steffan! How's it going?"

A man in his mid-to-late twenties was jogging towards Zack, seemingly pleased to see him.

"Zack, my old friend!" They embraced, lightly slapping each other's backs. "It's good to see you, man."

"You too, it's been a while." He pulled back. "This is Jenny, my girlfriend. Jenny, Steffan's dad used to manage the estate for both villas. I haven't seen him for a couple of years."

"It's nice to meet you." I held out my hand to him, but he pulled me in for a hug instead.

"It's great meeting you," he said. "I hope you are enjoying our island."

"Steffan and his family were originally from mainland Greece," Zack said to me. "But they moved across to Crete when he was younger. So, if you want to know anything at all about Crete, this is your guy." Zack looked so pleased to be reunited with him. "I can't believe you're here, this is so random."

"Ah, not so random, my friend, I am working on the boats today to help out. Not yours, unfortunately, I just brought a group across. I can't stay, but when I saw you I had to come across and say hello."

"I'm glad you did. Will we see you at the villa? You could come by for a drink, or–"

"Steffan!" an older Greek man by the boats shouted across to him.

"Sorry, I'm going to have to…"

"Don't apologise," Zack reassured him. "It was great seeing you. We're here for another week, if you get a chance to come over at all."

"I'll try." Steffan put his hands on his hips. "I want to, but you know how it–"

"Steffan!" the man shouted again.

"Go on," Zack said. "We'll catch up another time."

Steffan nodded and slowly walked away to the angry man who had been bellowing his name loudly enough for the whole island to hear.

"What was that about?" I asked as soon as he was out of earshot.

"That was his dad shouting to him."

"The one who managed the estate? Why didn't he come over, if he knows you too?"

Zack put his arm around me and led us to our boat, which had started to fill up. We would be able to get a seat, but unfortunately there would be no shade. Once again, I was grateful for the hat.

"It's a long story and I don't want to speculate too much, as I wasn't there when it all kicked off. All I know is there was a huge falling out between him and Chloe's parents. My parents tried to calm the situation, but Steffan's dad really wasn't happy. They quit immediately and I haven't seen Steffan properly in a long time. It's quite complicated. I'll try to explain it better sometime. Come on, hop aboard, m'lady."

CHAPTER EIGHTEEN

The day after our excursion to Spinalonga, we had planned to have another trip to the beach. Zack and I were going to take a picnic and our own deckchairs so we could spend the day there again, but the weather had different ideas. The beautiful blue sky had disappeared completely. Clouds in a multitude of colours covered the sky, threatening to unleash the fiery wrath of Zeus, so all four of us decided to stay indoors where it was safe. By late afternoon, the sky was almost black.

"The storms here are something else," Zack said as we stood right by the open sliding doors, gazing out. It was still quite warm, but I suspected the rain would descend very soon and cool things down. "Dad, when was it that we lost power for days after that *huge* storm?"

"Oh, a few years ago now. You were just a teen, I think." He joined us to look outside. "Lightning struck just up there, on that hill where the powerline is. Knocked it off for three days. Some holidayers packed up and went home early."

"Wow," I said. "Could that happen again?"

"No," Alistair assured me. "After that happened, they installed a backup system. They don't want holidaymakers being put off by the thought of no electricity. If it ever does go out now, it's not for long. Oh, wait, did you hear that?"

We fell silent. There was another rumble in the distance.

"You might want to close those doors," Miranda said. "It won't be long now."

As though the mighty god Zeus could hear her, the clouds finally unleashed the rain and I had never seen or heard anything like it. I jumped back as Alistair and Zack quickly slid the doors shut and the rain battered down on the patio.

I never thought anywhere could rain harder than back home in the north of England. But I was mistaken. The swimming pool was no longer visible as rainwater splashed everywhere. Having the doors closed helped with the noise, but we could still hear it hitting the canopy with force.

"I hope everyone is hungry," Miranda said. "I've made a pasta bake, and there's more than I thought there would be. I'm terrible with measurements. Should we invite Stan and Bev over?"

"I think we can let them look after themselves tonight," Alistair quickly responded.

"Good idea," Miranda agreed. "Jenny, I don't think I can apologise enough for Beverley's behaviour the other night. That poor Chloe, the things she puts up with."

The pasta bake smelled amazing. Miranda was right, it was large. Probably enough food to feed a family of ten. She carried it over to the dining table, and I picked up the plates and followed her.

I jumped as thunder cracked above us as I was setting out the plates, grateful I didn't drop any on the floor. Although, when in Greece...

"That was close," Miranda said, glancing up to check the doors were firmly shut.

"Fairly." Alistair was still standing by the door, looking out onto the hills. "Few miles away, but I think it's heading over to us now. I should have pulled the furniture in. It'll be everywhere if the wind picks up."

"Well, hopefully it passes quickly. Come on, everyone. Let's sit down and eat. You kids can tell us what you've been up to."

Miranda proudly placed the food in the centre of the table. Zack laid out the cutlery beside each plate, sneakily kissing my cheek as he passed me when his parents weren't looking. Alistair pulled out a bowl of salad from the fridge and we all sat together. The food was so delicious that I couldn't resist a second helping.

"So, Jenny," Miranda had finished her own second helping of pasta, "I was thinking, if you and Zack didn't have plans tomorrow, how about you and I go shopping then?"

"I'd love to." I looked to Zack. "Is that okay with you?"

"Of course it is." He smiled and put his arm around me. "We have plenty of time left to do our beach day. I think I might need a day in bed after eating this much pasta anyway. That was good though, Mum. Thank you."

"Yes, thank you. I'd eat another portion if I thought I wouldn't burst." My stomach was solid. I probably shouldn't have had all that bread with it. If Zack wanted sex tonight, there was no chance of me going on top. I doubted I could even make it up the stairs, let alone trying anything more athletic.

"I'm so pleased you enjoyed it. And I'm so excited to shop with you, too. There are some really nice–"

We all jumped as thunder and lightning clapped above us. It sounded like a bomb had blasted into the ceiling. Unfortunately, it knocked off the electrics, leaving us sitting in darkness.

"Oh, the torches, Alistair. Where did we put them?"

"Under the sink." Alistair slid his seat back. "Wait there, everyone."

"Here, Dad, take this." Zack switched on the torch on his phone and handed it to Alistair so he could see where he was going.

"Thanks, I'll get some candles too."

We sat in almost pitch black, straining to see Alistair as he wandered into the kitchen and fumbled under the sink. Eventually, two giant orbs of light emerged from the darkness. He handed Zack one of the torches and placed two smaller ones on the table.

"I could only find these," he said, placing a small tub on the table, which contained a bag of tea-lights and a lighter.

"We can use this." Miranda brushed the breadcrumbs from her side plate and pulled a few of the candles from the tub. Once lit, they created a really nice ambiance. "There we go, much better." She smiled. It really was lovely.

"Oh, I forgot to say," Zack began, "we saw Steffan and his dad yesterday. They're working on the tourist boats over at Spinalonga."

"Really? I don't suppose his dad was hospitable?" Alistair asked.

"No, not really. He..."

Another loud crack of thunder interrupted Zack, and then there was a chaotic mixture of screams and calling out in panic as the flash of lightning revealed a silhouette of a person at the sliding doors, banging to get inside.

"Oh my goodness, let her in!" Miranda said, as Zack recovered from having screamed in such a high-pitched way, and I tried not to laugh at him in front of his parents. Alistair rushed to the door to let in a soaking-wet Chloe.

"Thank you, oh, thank you so much." She wiped the rain from her face. "Isn't it horrible outside?" She was wearing an oversized white T-shirt, and evidently little else. It was clinging to her cold, wet skin.

"What an earth were you doing out there?" Zack asked, as she pulled out a chair and sat down next to him.

"I had to get away." She shook her head. "Dad's somehow sleeping through this noise so Mum has been nagging me and then she started shouting. I'm pretty sure Dad is faking it just for some peace."

She looked like she'd been crying. I was starting to feel sorry for her, and was just about to offer to lend her some of my dry clothes, maybe even a conservative dressing gown, but then she leaned across and put her head on Zack's shoulder.

"It's so hard being here sometimes. I just need a hug."

"You poor love," Miranda said. "Don't you worry, stay here tonight. The room next to Zack and Jenny is empty, so you can stay in there."

"That would be amazing. Thank you, guys. You're the best. Is that the room we all crashed in the other year?" She directed the question to Zack.

"Yes, it is." He shuffled awkwardly in his seat.

They all crashed together? All who? Why didn't Zack crash in his own room? Who else was there? Was it just the two of them?

"I'll be back in a minute," I said, grateful that the dim glow of the candles was hiding my burning cheeks.

"Everything okay?" Zack asked.

"Yes, I just want to check my phone. I left it on charge earlier. I won't be long."

I picked up the torch and found my way upstairs to the bedroom, closing the door behind me. I tried to compose myself for a few minutes, fighting the images of Zack and Chloe crashing on a bed together during previous summer vacations here.

My phone pinged from the bedside table, pulling me out of

my panic. I followed the glow of the screen and picked it up to read the message.

> Hey, haven't heard from you and was getting worried… How's it going? Call me if you need to (conversation still paused) (still love you) (you were right about Bing, he's a knob) Xxx

I couldn't help but laugh at the last part and wondered what on earth he had done now.

> Hey, can't call but can give a quick update… I'm so bothered by the twenty-something, she's here now dressed like a competitor in a wet T-shirt competition, cuddling up to Zack and talking about how they all used to crash together in bed!!! 🙁 xxx

> She's got a nerve!!! What is she thinking?? How's he reacting? And wet T-shirt? Xx

> We've got a ridiculous storm going on at the moment and she was out in it… TBF he isn't exactly encouraging her. He looked a bit awkward.

> Well, it sounds innocent on his side. Are you okay? Xx

> I will be, just needed a moment to myself. What has Bing done?

> I moved his litter box from the kitchen to the bathroom, but he didn't like that and when I got home from work he had pooped in the kitchen sink!! I thoroughly bleached it, but now can't bring myself to wash up in there… I've got a dishwasher on order. Xx

My final message to her was just a few dozen laughing emojis. That cat's got my back.

~

The storm eventually passed through the night and by morning, the blue sky I had come to know and love had returned. Although it felt chillier than usual, Alistair assured me it was forecast to be hot again by noon.

"What are you getting up to this morning while I'm out with your mum?" I asked Zack as we sat and had breakfast together out on the patio. The outdoor furniture was still too wet to sit on, so we took two of the dining chairs out.

"Not much, probably chill with my dad." There was no mention of Chloe, which was a relief. She'd disappeared first thing before we got up. "Are you sure you're all right? You look pale." He leaned close and put his arm around me. "If you're not feeling up to it, my mum won't mind. She won't be offended if you just want to hang out here for the day. There's plenty of time to shop."

"I'm fine, honestly. Don't worry."

He pulled my face towards his and placed a kiss on my non-responsive lips.

"You'd tell me though, right? If something was wrong, if something was bothering you?"

"Of course, it's all good. I must just be tired from all the heat. Not used to it. I just need some retail therapy and I'll be fine this afternoon."

"Are you sure?"

"Yeah, I'm sure." I smiled, possibly unconvincingly.

"Good morning, campers!" Miranda came out to the patio. In her white shorts, blue blouse and straw hat, she was ready for a girls' day out. "Zacky, don't let your father sit inside watching the telly with Stan all day. He needs some vitamin D. Make sure he sits outside for a while. In fact, get them both cleaning up, the storm has caused a bit of a mess." The pool was full of floating leaves and the cushions from the loungers had scattered.

"Will do, Mum."

"Are you all right, Jenny? You look quite pale."

"She doesn't look right, does she? I'm worried. Are you sure you're up for it today?" Zack looked really concerned, but I didn't feel up to talking about it just now. It would have to be tonight.

"I promise I'm okay." I stood up, brushing the crumbs from my breakfast onto my plate. "It was a rough night, what with the noise of the storm on the roof, but a girly day is what the doctor ordered."

"I'm glad to hear it." She genuinely looked happy to be heading out with me. I guess with having only a son, she missed out on these things.

"I thought we were going to Elounda?" I asked as we took the short trip in a taxi down the road to Agios Nikolaos instead, winding around the compact roads and over the little bridge.

"Oh, I changed my mind, is that all right? There are more shops here, so I thought it'd be more fun for us."

"That's fine." I could finally look in all the little shops and spend some money. That would take my mind off things. "I love looking at all the handmade jewellery."

"Well, let's see what we can buy to fill up our suitcases. We have all day. Zack will be busy getting things ready."

"Ready for what?"

"Oh, didn't he tell you? He's useless sometimes, that boy." She laughed, shaking her head. "It's our thirty-fifth wedding anniversary today."

"Oh wow, congratulations!" I beamed. They'd been married for longer than I'd been alive. What a crazy thought that was.

"Yes, we thought we'd have a special dinner tonight. We planned it last night, while you were upstairs. Very last minute."

My stomach flipped. Another dinner with Beverley the drunken witch, and Chloe her trampy daughter, and the husband who sits quietly and lets it all happen. Just what I needed. "It'll only be the four of us, so a little bit more intimate."

Phew.

"That sounds lovely. Well, if it is a special occasion, we have a *lot* of shopping to do."

We got out of the taxi and linked arms as we set off on our trip. It was already brightening my mood, and once again, I was doubting myself. Was Zack really being that inappropriate? Was it all actually only one-sided? Was I getting paranoid because I had finally found a guy I loved and wanted to spend my life with, and I was worried I might have chosen badly, just like my best friend did?

Two hours into our shopping trip, I had bought myself some gorgeous Greek jewellery, a mini statue of a minotaur, a new handheld fan (which I couldn't wait to show Zack) and I even got Sarah a little gift as a thank you. Even if our relationship was on the rocks, she had been looking after my cat, although I suspected this would be the last time she ever offered to cat-sit the demon feline.

"I just want to go back into that boutique before we eat, is that all right?" Miranda asked.

"Of course, go ahead. I'll wait outside." I sprung open my fan and began cooling myself. Alistair had been right about the heat returning. The boutique had no air conditioning and I couldn't face going back inside.

"Okay, I'll be two minutes. I might buy that dress after all."

I watched as she went in and was welcomed back by the shop assistant who spoke perfect English. I pulled out my phone. There were no further messages from Sarah, so I decided to see what was happening in the world of social media.

Curiosity got the better of me so I searched for my new favourite twenty-something.

Her Instagram profile was public, as she was clearly a budding influencer, so it was easy to find her. I just went into Zack's list of followers and chose the only one whose username contained anything close to 'Chloe'. I scrolled through her recent posts, most of which were of her in suggestive poses, wearing a barely-there bikini. Each photo had nearly a hundred likes.

I did a double take and scrolled back up to the top. The latest post, from today, twenty minutes ago, was a selfie of Chloe and *my* boyfriend. The same boyfriend who clearly lied to me and told me he would be at the villa all day, with his dad. My mouth went dry and I felt a ringing in my ears as I looked at their faces, grinning and pressed together, and read the caption.

Day out with Z, exciting things to come. x

What the... is he spending the day with her? Where are they? What are they doing? Why wouldn't he have told me about it? He actively lied! Why did he even bring me on holiday if he was just wanting to spend the days with her? Was he splitting his time between us?

I was fuming. My new fan almost crumpled under my rageful wafting. I didn't know whether I wanted to scream or cry.

And then I saw them.

As I looked up from my phone, there they were, linking arms, walking down the road, totally oblivious. But, of course, Zack had no idea we were going to be coming here today. Even I'd thought we were going to Elounda, which was in the opposite direction. They would have thought they'd be free from being discovered here. No girlfriend, no judgemental parents, they could do what they liked.

I watched from behind my fan as they walked into one of the shops. Zack held the door open for her, always a gentleman, and she stepped inside.

With my phone still in my hand, I wanted to call him, but instinct sent me somewhere else. I typed a message to Sarah.

> It's over. He's with her now, I've just seen them together. I'm with his mum, shopping. He lied to me so he could spend the day with her.

She replied almost instantly.

> OMG! Wanker! Can I call you? Xx

> If I talk about it, I'll cry, and I don't want his mum to see me upset. Can you see if there are any flights out for me tonight? The wifi here isn't great and I'm running low on data.

> I'll have a look, but please TALK to him tonight. He has no idea you're feeling like this. Promise me you'll talk to him. Then call me and, if you still want to, I will make sure you can get home Xx

I agreed with Sarah that I would hold off on making a dramatic exit until I had spoken to Zack. I would wait until after the anniversary dinner so I wouldn't ruin the night. But my heart was breaking. Having what should have been a fun lunch with Miranda, followed by celebrating a thirty-fifth wedding anniversary, was the last thing I needed right now.

CHAPTER NINETEEN

We were all seated around the outside dining table. Alistair had just cooked us a wonderful dinner, something I had never even thought of trying before, grilled lobster. My sister-in-law would have had a stroke had she witnessed the carnage, but it was delicious. With sides of roasted new potatoes, salad and coleslaw, it was amazing. Quite interesting the first time you snap into the lobster itself, but once you try it, you're in culinary heaven.

The food was great, but the tension at the table reeked of rotten shellfish. I was obviously quiet, given my devastating discovery earlier today, but Zack seemed to be acting funny too. Guilt, maybe? Could he sense that I knew? When we got back from shopping, I had asked him about his day, and he'd stuttered that he had been relaxing by the pool for most of it, reading a book. The lie cut right through my gut.

I just had to keep calm and cool until later on tonight. Once Miranda and Alistair had gone to bed, I would talk to him and find out what had been going on. It was time to ask the dreaded question, whether he had been cheating on me with Chloe. If he admitted it, could I ever forgive him?

"I'd like to make a toast." Zack stood up and his parents smiled. I'd never known him to make a speech before. His upper lip was sweating, and he looked nervous, I guessed he didn't always display words of affection in front of his parents. It was a special occasion, I suppose, but they were looking at him as though they'd been expecting this. "Mum, Dad, I'd like to wish you a very happy anniversary. You have been a huge inspiration, not only as parents but as a couple. If I can be even half as happy as you two are in thirty-five years then I'll know I've succeeded in life. There is nothing I want more." I could see a tear in his mum's eye. Then he turned to me. I was surprised he couldn't hear my heart pounding. "Jenny, I know I've been acting weird today, and maybe even for the last few days, but see, I had a plan. This last year has been the best, most exciting and enjoyable time of my life. I have fallen so deeply in love, I cannot imagine my life without you. So, Jenny..." He put down his glass and pulled a small box out of his pocket. Pushing back his chair, he got down on one knee in front of me and said... "Will you marry me?"

"Jenny?" I think Zack said my name, but I can't actually be sure. "Jenny, are you all right?"

I opened my mouth to speak, but could hardly form any words. I could hardly breathe. My mouth was so dry I almost retched. Marry him? He wants me to marry him? He and Chloe... The lies... What? "I thought... you and... I need some water."

"Alistair, dear, why don't we give these two a moment?" She and Alistair very quickly made their way inside the villa, sliding the doors closed behind them and pulling the curtains.

"Are you all right?" Zack was still on his knees in front of me, the box now open. I could see a beautiful white gold ring nestled inside. It had a diamond-studded band with a square-cut diamond in the centre looking up at me.

"I thought you and Chloe..." The tears caught in my throat, so I couldn't finish.

"Me and Chloe? What about us?"

"I saw you. The other day by the pool, she was on top of you, and you've been so close, and then today I saw you both in town, but then you lied, and..." I was so short of breath by now, my nose all stuffed from snot and tears wasn't helping. "I thought you were cheating on me." I'd finally said it.

Zack almost lost his balance.

"Cheating on you? I would never do that to you!" He stood up, pulled his chair right next to mine, and sat so that our legs were touching. He put his hand on my thigh. "Is that what you thought? I'm... I'm so sorry, but, no! I should probably have said the other day when we saw... but I didn't even think..."

"What?"

What was he going to tell me? Did they have a history? Did they sleep together last year but decide to stay friends? Were they friends with benefits before I came along?

"Chloe is in a serious relationship with Steffan. She has been for years."

"She... she what?"

"She's with Steffan." He was whispering. "That's what the fall-out was about between the parents. I wasn't here when it happened, but his dad was working on the estate, doing his inspections, and walked in on them both together. He was furious."

"She's... she and Steffan?" I was still struggling to understand, given the set ideas I'd had in my head.

"Yes," he grabbed both my hands, "that's why she's out here. She would never choose to holiday with her parents, they all drive each other up the wall. But it's the only way they can spend any time together. They're completely in love."

"So, the other day when she jumped on you..." I pointed

across to the sun loungers where I had seen them both sitting together, whispering.

"When you nipped upstairs, she was asking me all about you. Wanting the juicy details. And when I told her that I was planning to do this, she jumped on me all giddy and excited. She really likes you and is so happy for us."

"But you seem so close," I said, thinking about how she liked to grab him, hug him, lean on him in a soaking wet T-shirt, leaving very little to the imagination.

"She's like my little sister, of course we're close. And I am so sorry you thought something else. I'm mortified. She would be too. She'd say, 'That's so gross', and pretend to vomit."

I couldn't help but laugh at his impression.

"But today, you lied. You were with her, and said you were here. I saw you."

I still felt like there were so many questions which needed to be answered.

"Chloe collared me as I was on my way out to collect the ring from a jewellery shop in town. I had ordered it a few weeks ago, my parents were already here so they helped to facilitate it. Chloe had plans to meet Steffan for lunch, but if her mum saw her going out alone she would have interrogated her. So, she asked if she could tag along to make it look like an innocent outing. She came with me to pick up the ring."

I thought back to her Instagram post, *Day out with Z, exciting things to come. x.* Now it all made sense.

"You planned to propose all this time?" Reality was setting in. He had been planning this for weeks.

"Yes. I wanted to be traditional and get your parents' permission, but with your dad not being here, and things with your mum being up and down, I called your brother and he and I had a good talk."

Andrew. That's why he was at my house that day.

"You asked Andrew for permission to marry me?" The tears were back, but they weren't angry tears. They weren't even sad tears.

"Yes." Zack's eyes were filling with tears too. "I called him asking if we could chat. You were still out, and he wasn't too far away, so he came over. We had a really good chat and I promised at the wedding to slip some cocktail sausages into his tofu, so naturally he said he approved."

I laughed, a much-needed one. My body relaxed as he laughed with me, holding my hands. He was crying too.

"So, Jenny," he wiped his eyes, and whilst still on one knee, he reopened the small box, "I'm asking again. Will you marry me?"

CHAPTER TWENTY

I pulled up outside Sarah's house, ready to collect Bing and see how much compensation Sarah wanted for damages to her new home. I had her gift from Crete in a little bag, as well as a bottle of kitchen cleaner and some wine. As long as he hadn't touched her sofa, we would probably be able to get away with it.

Sarah and I hadn't spoken properly since my mini meltdown in Agios Nikolaos. I was very nervous to see her. She had texted me a few times, asking if I was all right, but I hadn't replied. Not until this morning, when I asked what time I could pick Bing up.

"Hey." She tried to smile as she opened the door, but she was clearly nervous too. As she stepped to one side, I went in and looked around. There was no clear damage that I could see. Bing hadn't clawed at any of the newly painted walls, which was a huge relief. "Shall I put the kettle on?"

"I think you should."

She already had the cups prepared, and the kettle had not long since been boiled, so didn't take too long to be ready. We were both silent as the teaspoon clinked against the cups and

Sarah stirred the milk. She carried the cups back into the living room and I followed her. We sat apart on the sofa.

"I'm ready to talk about... about you and Dan," I finally said, breaking the silence.

She exhaled. I could tell she had a speech prepared. "I am so, so, so, so sorry. Dan and I weren't even meant to happen. I'd arranged a date with a different guy, who didn't show up. No message or anything, just completely ghosted me. It was the postman. I shouldn't have bothered. Anyway, as I was leaving the bar, I saw Dan." She broke off to look at me, but I said nothing. "I swear on my mother's life it was not pre-arranged, just pure chance. We had a drink, we had a laugh. Apparently, he'd seen me on the dating app too, but wasn't sure if it was appropriate to reach out, although he'd wanted to. We decided to have a kind of date, there and then..." She stopped and took a much-needed breath. "And Jenny, we really hit it off. We spoke on the phone. We texted. We went out again. I just..." Her hand covered her mouth, to stop her lip from quivering. "If I'd known." Her voice went high. "If I'd known it would cause this between us, I never would have..."

I leapt towards my crying friend and pulled her close. I couldn't stand seeing her like this. It wasn't worth it. "Please don't cry. It's okay." I hadn't seen her crying like this since the bombshell news about Max The Wanker becoming a dad.

"No, it isn't." She pulled back. "I kept it from you. You and I don't keep things from one another. It was really shitty of me. I don't know why I kept it from you. It was stupid!" She wiped her eyes with her sleeves. "I was being so selfish."

"Sarah, look, it was a big thing. I get it. I was hurt you couldn't talk to me. But barely speaking to you for two weeks has hurt me even more than that. I need you. Clearly," I said, thinking back to my almost Greek tragedy.

"I need you too, so I spoke to Dan and we might be calling it off."

"What on earth for?"

"I told him my friendship with you was more important. We've been together since we were eighteen. We've seen it all with each other. And after Max The Wanker, you pulled me back from the brink. I owe you everything."

That was it. We were both crying now. We hugged and soaked each other's shoulders with tears that had been a long time coming. But I was not losing my friend over a guy, and she was not losing a perfect guy over me.

"Sarah, you're not going to stop seeing him, do you hear me?" I pulled back and held on to her shoulders. Her blonde hair was stained dark from the tears. "Do you like him? I mean, really like him?"

"I do."

"Then, there you go. If you guys are happy, and if you're perfect for each other, it would be stupid to end it. To be honest, I think you'd be great together."

"I don't want things to be awkward though. I mean, you and he... Would it be weird for you? For Zack, if we all went out together?"

"It's all history. I promise. Besides... Oh, hello you. You finally came to say hello." I stroked Bing's head. He was chuntering under his breath, which was his way of saying, *"Where the hell have you been?"* "We need to get your stuff together and compensate Aunty Sarah for her condemned kitchen sink."

Bing jumped up on the couch and sniffed at my fingers, before stepping on me and rubbing himself on my black T-shirt, leaving a trail of white hair.

"When are you seeing Dan next then?" I asked Sarah.

"I'll text him in a bit. I think he's expecting me to call it off, so it'll hopefully be a nice surprise when I say otherwise. Are you sure it's going to be okay?"

"Yes, I'm sure. I promise. I'm so glad you've found someone decent. Before I went away, you seemed happier. I thought it was because you were getting rid of me for a while, but I guess there was another reason."

"I haven't felt this happy in ages. When he texts me, I get all giddy. Just like you did when Zack would message you in the early days. And, that day you found us, that was the first time we'd... you know."

"Oh, I was witness to a milestone!" I laughed. "I'm glad I can be a part of *that* memory. You opted to avoid the waterbed then?"

"Jenny, honestly, if this is going to be weird, I will end things with him."

"You're not going to end things with him. You're going to need him around in about twelve months' time."

"Why's that?"

"You'll need a date. Oh, didn't I tell you?"

"Tell me what?"

"I can't believe it slipped my mind." With my left hand, I rubbed my forehead. "How could I forget to tell her? Bing, I think I'm losing my memory, forgetting something so huge."

"Wait," she said, as she glanced at my finger. "Is that a...?"

"Oh, this?" I held out my left hand, clearly displaying the most beautiful engagement ring in the history of jewellery. "Yeah, Zack gave it to me in exchange for promising to be his wife."

"Ahhhh!" Our tea spilled all over her new couch as she launched herself at me, hugging me. Bing zoomed away in a panic. Sarah examined the ring as I told her everything that had happened on the night of the anniversary dinner.

I pulled a small bag from my pocket and handed it to Sarah,

watching her pull out a handmade bracelet made of silver, encrusted with green gems. "Will you be my maid of honour?"

"Jenny," her voice broke, "I would love to be your maid of honour." We held each other tightly for what felt like ages, glad to be back in each other's lives.

"I'm appointing myself chief wedding planner too. We have so much to plan!" Sarah bounced up from the couch, retrieving a notepad and pen from the kitchen. "We need wedding-dress shops, florists, venues, photographers... I'm pretty sure a few of my suppliers would offer me a discount, what with the amount of money they received from me for nothing in return, if you want me to call some of them? I can send you links to their webpages so you can see what you guys think."

"Absolutely, thanks!" I was full of confidence in Sarah's planning abilities. Once she was on a mission, there was no stopping her. "So, what else has been happening whilst I've been away?"

"So much, I don't know where to start." Sarah dropped the notepad in her lap, her expression suddenly looking less than enthusiastic. "Alessandro."

"What about him? Is he still in touch?"

"Not anymore! It all kicked off. He kept texting and calling, which was great at first, but then he began to get a little bit possessive."

"Really?" He had seemed so gentle and caring when we'd met him. "What did he do?"

"He kept hinting for me to go back out for a visit, which would have been so nice. I said someday I'd like to, but then he kept insisting. As though I could just pack up and hop on a plane and forget about work. It's just so easy, *right?*" she said in an exaggerated Italian accent. "Then I was out with Dan one evening. My phone kept ringing. He was trying to video-call me!"

"Eek, not awkward at all. What did Dan say?"

"Well, I'd told him about you and I going to Rome. I was honest about it all. No point in pretending to be all innocent. We're in our thirties, right? We have a past. He could see I was bothered though, so suggested I take the call, to get it over with." She paused.

"What happened?"

"His temper! *'You out with somebody? Tell me, tell me!'.* Luckily, the bar we were in was busy and so it was loud, so no one could really hear him. Anyway, Dan took the phone. Did you know he could speak Italian?"

"Where did he learn that?"

"His grandma, apparently. She was Italian. I can't believe you didn't know." I chose not to remind her that Dan and I never really spent time communicating when we were together. It was more of a physical thing. "Anyway, I haven't heard from him again since."

"Wow, Dan to the rescue." I smiled.

"And there's other news," she said, coyly.

"I'm listening..."

"I saw Max."

"*No!*" Bing, who had bravely returned to the living room, scarpered once again at my outburst. Nice to know he'd be on hand in an emergency. "When? Did he see you?"

"Yes, I saw him first. Pulled up behind him at the petrol station. Didn't even realise it was him because... Now, I want to be classy. We're all adults, decisions were made, and we must be mature. That being said, he looked rough. Not just 'new parent' rough. He looked like a completely different person, and not in a good way. He was driving this old, rusty car. No idea what happened to his old one, but there was no way he'd be seen dead in a car like that a few years ago."

"Did he speak to you?"

"No, but he saw me. I'd just come from a meeting so was suited and booted. He looked mortified, so embarrassed." She paused again. "Jenny, I know it's immature, but I made some terrible gestures at him. I don't think he's been left in any doubt about how I feel towards him."

"Sod being mature," I decided. "Serves him bloody right."

"You know the best bit though? Seeing him like that, it was strange. For the first time since we broke up, I realised I really am over him. I don't think I'd care if he turned up on my doorstep tomorrow, begging for me back!"

I laughed and hugged her tightly. "Oh, I've missed you. Please can we never break up again?"

"Definitely. Anyway, we have things to do."

"Indeed we do. Except..." I flashed my engagement ring in her direction. "I have no idea where to start."

"Don't you worry. I'll kick off bridesmaid duties and put together a list of jobs. And I shall crack on with the most important job of all."

"What's that?"

"The hen do!"

"Don't plan anything huge. I'm an old woman now. Just something sensible close to home. No naked men serving onion rings on their penises." Although, the thought of putting my mother through that made it tempting.

"Nah, I know what we're doing for your hen do. And it is just perfect."

"What?"

Sarah was the best party planner, so she would come up with something fantastic, I was sure.

"A long weekend... in Zante!" She screeched with laughter.

This renewed friendship might not last very long.

THE END

A NOTE FROM THE PUBLISHER

Thank you for reading this book. If you enjoyed it please do consider leaving a review on Amazon to help others find it too.

We hate typos. All of our books have been rigorously edited and proofread, but sometimes mistakes do slip through. If you have spotted a typo, please do let us know and we can get it amended within hours.

info@bloodhoundbooks.com